Ryker's ENCHANTMENT
HONEY CREEK DEN BOOK 3

TAYLOR RYLAN

Jay,
Get ready to
fall in love with
Ryker & Arin.
Hugs
Taylor Rylan

Copyright © 2018 by Taylor Rylan

Published in the United States by Taylor Rylan

All rights reserved. No part of this book may be reproduced, copied, or transmitted in any format or by any means without the prior written permission from the author.

This book is a work of fiction. Names, characters, places, and events are a product of the author's imagination. Any similarities to actual persons, living or dead, is pure coincidence. As are any similarities to any businesses, events or locations.

All products and brand names mentioned are registered trademarks of their respective holder and or company. I do not own the rights to these, nor do I claim to.

Cover Design by Jay Aheer of Simply Defined Art

Caution

This is a gay romance that contains the following:
Adult language, adult situations, explicit sexual material between two men over the age of 18. Guy parts are seriously going to be touching, knotting, and vibrating. This book is intended for **ADULTS ONLY**.

Note to Readers

I just want to first say thanks for giving my take on shifters a chance. In my world, shifters live multiple centuries and only knot and reproduce with their fated mate. Mates can be found anywhere, and you'll meet many multiple species couples in my world. I hope you enjoy Ryker and Arin's story.

Ryker — 1

The last thing I wanted to do when asked if I'd be willing to leave Kodiak and move to Montana was actually do so. But my bear pushed me for some reason, so I gave in. After all, he'd never led me wrong in the past.

I enjoyed my life as a park ranger, but I didn't want to leave my team that I had in Alaska. That was, until I arrived in Montana and discovered that I'd be working with only two other rangers, both shifters. Their Alpha, War, was more than willing to accept me into his den and for that I was grateful.

But my bear was driving me crazy. On more than one occasion while at Alpha War's place, he'd smelled something that was alluring. I hoped it meant our mate was close by, but I wasn't holding my breath. I was still fairly young, only one hundred thirty-nine. Yeah, I'd have loved to have met my mate by now, but at least I wasn't well over two-hundred like others. The few times I'd been to Alpha's house, it had been hit or miss. Sometimes I smelled the amazing scent, others, nothing.

So who knew what I was going to encounter when I showed up for the celebration of Troy's triplets having been born. I was ecstatic for the mated pair. Troy was an excellent ranger, and I was thankful I didn't lose him because of his suddenly much-larger family. He worked shorter hours now that his mate Elliot had given birth to their boys, but I had no complaints. He was good at what he did, and when he was at work, he put in more than one hundred percent.

When I parked my truck and got out, my bear pushed at me to hurry around the house and get to the party. What was wrong with him? When I made it halfway around the house, I was suddenly hit with a scent that made my cock go instantly hard and my bear yell *Mate! Ours!* I couldn't stop the loud growl that escaped, nor would I have wanted to.

By the time I made it to the back of the house, my bear was ready to burst free and run up to our mate. I fought him back and convinced him to stay put. At least for now. There would be plenty of time for him to get to know our mate on a more personal level once I'd claimed him.

I zeroed in on the beautiful red-head that was talking to Wallace and a family of fox shifters. He looked almost exactly like Alpha Mate Arik so I had to assume he was his twin that I hadn't met, yet. And if memory recalls, Arik's twin was a warlock, not a shifter. I could live with that. Elliot is a warlock and Troy had mentioned that there were certainly benefits to it.

When I walked towards my mate, I saw nobody but him and couldn't take my eyes off of the young man. Unfortunately, when I got within several feet of him and was about to introduce myself, he vanished. Shocked, I immediately looked to Wallace, but after he gave me an apologetic look, he too disappeared. I looked around the party and when I found Troy walking to me, I had to wonder what was going on.

"Did I do something wrong?"

"I don't think so. I was talking to Edison when it happened. He said Wallace called out through their bond for help, and then they went after Arin to see what the problem was."

"Does he not want me for a mate? I realize I'm a shifter and not a warlock, but right now, my bear is tearing me apart wanting answers."

"I understand, Ryker. And just as soon as they find out, I know they'll be back and let you know."

I was falling apart on the inside. My bear wanted to break free and run after our mate to find out what he could do to fix whatever was wrong. Did my growling scare him? Was he ashamed that his mate was a shifter? Did he already have a lover that he preferred?

When Edison reappeared, he walked right to me and gave me a forced smile.

"Ryker. Perhaps it would be best if we went somewhere private to talk?"

"What? No. He doesn't want me, does he?"

"I'm sorry, Ryker. Arin is young and he's—"

My heart broke right then and there. My mate—after finally finding him—didn't want me. I couldn't contain the heart-wrenching bellow that escaped my throat before I took off towards the back of the property. I shifted mid-run, shredding my clothes along the way. By the time I reached the tree line, I was at a full-out run and didn't stop until I was miles away from War's house by a small creek.

I quickly drank my fill, laid down, and simply gave up. My bear was just as broken-hearted as I was. Our mate, our beautiful mate, didn't want us. What was it about us that he found distasteful?

After I laid there for who knows how long, I got up and decided now was as good of a time as any to start my trek back to my place. Since I lived in a cabin near the ranger station I worked at, it was several more miles before I smelled my territory. I detected no humans in the area so when I arrived in my own backyard, I quickly shifted. After retrieving the spare key I had hidden on the back deck, I let myself inside.

Looking around, I realized that the happy home I'd made for myself here in Montana would all be a memory. There was no way

I'd be able to stay here knowing my mate would be back and wasn't interested. My bear would eventually go insane. After a long, hot shower, I put on a pair of sweatpants and went to my home office to write up my request for transfer. It was going to be hell waiting for a new assignment, but it was something both me and my bear would need.

After typing up the request, I went to hit send but my computer froze. Damn thing. Of course, it did. Could anything else go wrong today? Really? I decided it was better to just go to bed and try resending the request tomorrow from my work computer.

I was momentarily sidetracked by loud banging on my door, that could only be more bad news, and I chose to ignore it. Luckily, whoever was at the door eventually gave up and left. Or so I thought. Just as I was about to climb the stairs, Arin, my disappearing mate, fell from the middle of the room and landed in a heap right next to me.

"Are you okay?" I asked as I went to help him up off of the floor.

"Yeah, I've had several reentries that were worse. Although, if you'd just answered your door, I could've walked in."

"I wasn't aware that it was you on the other side. You want to tell me what you're doing here? I thought you weren't interested in being my mate. You disappeared when I approached you."

"I know. And I'm sorry. Can we maybe talk?"

I noticed Arin staring at my chest, and it was then that I remembered I hadn't put on a shirt after my shower earlier. Hmm, interesting. Perhaps my little mate wasn't quite as disinterested as I first thought? My bear was screaming at me to grab our mate and claim him before he could leave again, and I told him to shut up and have some patience. He huffed and growled at me, but I chose to ignore him.

"Yeah, we can talk. How about we go have a seat on the couch? Or would you be more comfortable at the table? Either works for me."

"The couch is fine."

"Alright. Follow me." I quickly turned and headed to my rarely used den, and after Arin plopped down on one end of the couch, I took the other. I made sure the entire length of the couch was between us. I didn't want him to feel as if I was crowding him or pressuring him. I just sat there and stared at my beautiful mate. Even though he'd all but refused me, I couldn't help it; he was simply stunning, and my bear and I still wanted him. Always would. No matter what happened, he would be it for me for the rest of my life. I looked at Arin and hoped like hell he didn't reject me a second time. If he did, I knew I wouldn't survive.

"I'm so sorry, Ryker. I get nervous easily, and when I do, I tend to just teleport away. I don't want to hurt you, and I know if we claim each other that's what'll happen because I'm so accident prone. I'm still working on mastering my powers, and I thought I had more time. It's almost unheard of for a warlock to find their One when they're as young as I am, but now, here you are. And I don't want anything to happen to you. I could never live with myself if I hurt you, and that's why I ran away. I didn't want to cause you any kind of pain, and see, that's what I ended up doing anyway."

"Arin!" I sternly called my mate's name, effectively cutting off his rambling. Thank fates for that. I didn't know if he'd ever stop. I saw a shiver go through his body and promised myself that I'd address that later. But for now, I needed some answers.

"Are you okay?" I asked as I moved closer and gently placed a hand on his arm. He jerked and pulled away, and I did my best to not feel hurt, but I couldn't. It hurt so much that I was almost positive he saw the hurt in my eyes before I could mask it. I quickly moved back to the other side of the couch.

"I'm okay, thank you for asking."

"Do you always ramble non-stop?"

"Only when nervous."

"Why do I make you nervous? You're my mate, Arin. I could never hurt you. You should know that. Is it because I'm a bear and not a warlock?"

"What? No! I already told you. I don't want to hurt you. And I already have, more than once."

"Okay, let's start from the beginning, okay? Hi, I'm Ryker. I'm very pleased to meet you." I extended my hand and waited for Arin to either take it or simply disappear again. Thankfully, he gently placed his slim hand in mine, and I swear I felt a vibration go through me.

"Hi Ryker. I'm Arin, as you know. I'm a warlock, but you know that too. I'm still trying to master something as basic as teleporting, and there's so much more that I still need to learn besides that. I'm scared that I'm going to hurt you. I hurt everyone that I try teleporting somewhere."

"Is that the only reason? Is there something else? If it's just the fact that you can't teleport…"

"I don't want to hurt you! You don't understand. No matter how much I practice, no matter how many times I'm talked through it, it doesn't work. I seem to lose focus in the middle of it and we land in a heap somewhere. Sometimes, nowhere near the intended destination."

"Okay. So do you want to wait until you master teleporting? Or longer? I need to know what's going on in your head. I'm almost a hundred and forty. I've only ever teleported a couple times with your brother and Edison. Is it the only thing keeping us apart? As far as I'm concerned, it's not necessary. At least, not for me. I've always traveled the old-fashioned ways: walking, driving, or flying. Are you really going to reject our mating simply because you're afraid you'll hurt me while teleporting us somewhere?"

"I don't want to. Trust me, it hurt when I left you there without even saying hi. I cried so hard, Papa had to bring me here to your cabin. When you didn't answer, I obviously took more drastic measures to get inside. But, I never wanted to cause you pain."

"Trust me, mate, you're very much worth a little pain."

"What if I land on you when we fall?"

"Mmm, I can think of worse things than you landing on me."

Arin flushed bright red at that, and I loved that the idea of him being on top of me made him blush and squirm.

"You want to share with me what's going through your mind right now, mate? I like that blush. It's very cute."

"Umm, nothing? Can we maybe just talk for a little longer? I'd really like to get to know you better."

"I have to let you know, right now my bear is happy and content with just being near you. And the fact that you haven't disappeared and are willing to talk to me, makes us both happy. It hurt when you left so abruptly. No shifter likes to be rejected by their mate."

The gasp and look of horror on Arin's face had me both confused, yet, hopeful.

Arin — 2

He thought I was rejecting him? Shit! What else was he supposed to think? I left. Now I've gone and told him I didn't want to mate with him because I didn't want to hurt him. I was screwing this up completely.

"I'm sorry. I'm messing everything up. Would you rather I just left?"

"Oh, no. You're not getting out of this that easy. What's it going to take to convince you to consider accepting me?"

"What? You don't have to convince me. I accept you. I just dread the thought of hurting you, and I know that eventually I will."

"Wait. So, you're saying you're not rejecting me?"

"I never wanted to. I never intended for it to seem like that. I just panicked. Trust me when I say, I will somehow hurt you when I try to teleport us somewhere."

"So you're willing to be mine, as the fates wanted?"

"Oh, Ryker. I'd love to be yours. But I'm scared. I don't want to mess things up. It's going to be embarrassing for you to be mated to me. The warlock who can't teleport, among other things. I just learned to levitate objects not long ago. For whatever reason, things seem to be more difficult for me than they were for my brothers."

"Stop. There's nothing embarrassing about you. And everyone here knows you. Why would it be an issue? Honestly, I'm positive that with time you'll get the hang of it. Now, you mentioned that you were willing to be mine?"

"Are you kidding? Who wouldn't want to be yours? You're hot!" I could *not* believe I'd just blurted that out to my One. What was I? A teenager with his first crush?

"I'm glad you approve, mate. You're adorable, you know that?"

"Eep!" Shit! Did I seriously just squeak? What was wrong with me?

"Would you like to get to know each other better first? We have plenty of time. I can wait to claim you if you'd like. I'm sure if I let Troy know he'll cover for me tomorrow, and we can spend the day together."

"I'd like that very much. Should we go let him know then?"

"No, mate. It's late. He's probably curled up with your brother by now. I have a spare bedroom if you'd like to stay. If not, you can come back here tomorrow, or I can come to War's to see you."

"If you don't mind, can I stay in your spare room?"

"If I minded, I wouldn't have offered. Of course, you can. My bear is super happy you decided to stay here. I promise, no pressure whatsoever. I'm thankful you're not saying no to us just yet. And if you decide you can't be mated to me, I won't like it and it'll hurt, but I'll understand."

"That's not going to happen. But if I can have some time to get to know you a little better, and so you can see just what you're going to be up against, I'd feel better."

"Arin, there's no rush, truly. Now if you'll follow me, I'll show you to the spare room."

I nodded and walked behind Ryker's tall form. I tried to not stare at his body, but I couldn't help myself. It was gorgeous. He was tall and lean, but well defined. I could stare at him all day and still never get tired of looking at him. Now if I could only bring myself to say yes to our claiming each other.

Ryker saying we could take our time proved that he didn't know warlocks vibrate once they met their One. My body was already vibrating continuously. If Ryker didn't claim me within a few days, the vibrations would become downright painful, and it would become difficult for me to function. Hopefully, I'd be able to show him just how much of a mess-up I was before then. My brothers had all mastered everything by the time they were in their fifties. More than once, I'd been reminded that I was behind and had screwed up yet another simple task.

"Here we go. The sheets are clean and fresh. Honestly, I don't even know why I have a spare room, but now that you're here, I'm glad I do. It's nothing fancy—"

"It's perfect. Thank you. I don't need fancy. I'm not fussy and I'm not high maintenance. Promise."

"If you need me, my room is right there. Just knock and I'll hear you."

"Thanks, Ryker. I should be fine. I really do appreciate everything."

"It's no problem. This is what mates do, Arin. Have a good night."

"You too." I gently closed the door once Ryker turned away and started the short trip to his room at the end of the hallway. Turning back to the room he'd given me, I noticed it was neat and clean, but sparsely furnished. I had less than three days to make sure I was who Ryker wanted, and that he wasn't simply basing his decision on the fact the fates decided we were perfect for each other. I knew it wouldn't be easy to be mated to me, and I needed to know without a doubt that he was willing.

I flopped down on the bed and thought about Ryker. My One was so hot. Why would he ever want a screw-up like me? I was sure that if we claimed each other right away, he'd end up hurt and embarrassed. I couldn't even teleport properly, and that was easy for every other warlock.

Looking around, I realized there was only a closet in the room. I got up, and after venturing out to the hallway, found the bathroom, took care of my nighttime routine, and went back to the room and crawled between the sheets. Tomorrow morning I'd get a chance to show my One how much better off he'd be without me for a mate. Even if in the end, I was in too much pain to function.

I should have known that since my One and I had finally met, sleeping in his house without him beside me would be a challenge. I tossed and turned all night, and when the sun finally started peeking over the horizon and into the room, I gave up and got out of bed. With a thought, I was fully dressed in clean clothes. Thankfully, that was something that I had become skilled at. I quietly opened the door, so as not to wake Ryker, and went downstairs. I knew shifters had excellent hearing, but in the end, it was all unnecessary since he was sitting at his kitchen table when I entered.

"Good morning, Arin. Did you sleep well?"

"Not really, no. It wasn't the bed or anything, I just couldn't really fall asleep and stay that way. How about you?"

"Pretty much the same. My bear wasn't exactly happy that you weren't in bed with us last night. Don't worry, he'll get over it. Would you like some coffee?" Ryker picked up his mug and took another sip of the brew.

"Coffee sounds wonderful. If you let me know where—"

"Nope. Have a seat and I'll get it for you. How do you take it?"

"Usually hidden in copious amounts of creamer. But don't worry, I'll just…" I held up the container of creamer I'd conjured so he could see it.

"Where'd…you know, never mind. I don't need to ask where the creamer came from. I was about to say I didn't have any, but I guess it doesn't matter."

"Not really, no."

"Are you hungry? Do you want something to eat?"

"Not just yet. Maybe in a little while. Right now, I need my stomach to wake up a bit before I attempt to put food in it."

"Fair enough. Just let me know when you're hungry, and I'll gladly make you breakfast."

"You don't have to. I can make it. I can cook as well as conjure food. It's one of the few things that I can do all the time."

"If that's what you want to do, then I'll let you have at it. If you don't mind, I need to head to my home office for a few minutes. I have to give Troy a call, and I need to send a few emails out to the regional office. You're more than welcome to join me if you'd like. As my mate, even if we don't ever claim each other, I'll never have any secrets from you."

"I don't want to bother you though."

"You won't be. But do whatever's most comfortable for you."

I watched as Ryker got up, and I couldn't be sure, but I was almost positive I'd hurt him again. It seemed that no matter what I did, I was destined to cause him pain in some way. I knew that the emotional hurts could, and often did, cut deeper. I'd had to listen to my brothers pick on me for the past several years. It hurt. I knew they all loved me, but I also knew on some level, it embarrassed them that I couldn't do the simplest forms of magic.

Papa had encouraged me over and over, but it was no good. I kept screwing up. And it seemed the more I tried, the more frustrated I became and the more mistakes I made. It was a never-ending cycle. I decided it was probably better if I followed Ryker and just sat there and did nothing. Already, I felt calmer when I was near him. Except for the humming vibrations. Those were just becoming more intense as time went on. We still had a couple days before I'd need Papa's help. Hopefully, I could figure some things out before then.

I got up and followed the sound of Ryker's voice coming from an open doorway down the hall. I peeked my head in and he looked up from his desk. He smiled at me while motioning me into the office. Like everywhere else, it was tidy and neat. That didn't look promising for me. I was the king of making messes. With my magic not fully mastered, I tended to mess up a lot.

"Thanks, Troy. I'll be in touch." Ryker touched the screen of his phone and set it on the desk before looking up at me. "So, Troy said he'd be more than willing to cover for me for a few days. I just need to send out a report and an email, and I'm all yours. Sound good?"

"Yeah, thanks. But you didn't have to do anything like that. I could have just hung out with Arik or Elliot while you were at work."

"True, you could have. But then that wouldn't give us quite as much time to be together and get to know each other. This way, you'll get to know me quicker, and maybe I can convince you to be ours."

"That's not it, Ryker. I just...I don't know. I just don't want you to be laughed at because your mate is a bumbling warlock."

"Stop right there. There's nothing wrong with you. I don't know where you keep getting the idea that you're a screw-up, but it ends. Everyone has things they struggle with. Do you really think that all shifters have an easy time when they first learn to shift? We don't. In fact, there are lots of shifters that struggle well into adulthood to master shifting. We have it easy compared to you. We have to do one thing, shift. You have to learn and master all kinds of powers and things. That seems so much more difficult."

"Thank you," I replied before looking down at my lap. It was refreshing to hear someone say something nice. Especially since it was my One. Even if he technically wasn't mine yet.

"Arin, look at me, please?"

I looked up into Ryker's blue eyes, and my heart hurt at the look on his face. It was one of love, but I hadn't yet earned that from him. I knew my issues were my own, but I couldn't help it.

"While we're getting to know each other, we're going to work on your self-confidence. I don't know why it's lacking so much, but there isn't a reason for it. Yes, you're my mate, but even if you weren't, I'd still be able to tell that you were a wonderful and caring young man. I know what you did for Arik when you brought him here to meet War, as well as sharing your light with Edison after his fight with Arianna. Granted, I don't know a whole lot about your family, but Troy has mentioned a few things."

"I'm so happy Troy and Elliot found each other. And I adore their boys. I can't imagine three at once though. Elliot was miserable there at the end."

"Were you here for that?"

"Yes. I knew they'd need all the help they could get. And with Arik having twins of his own, he was already busy. But Dad and Papa fight over those boys, so I don't think they'll ever really want for a babysitter."

"Probably not. Troy's said how much help they've been. Let me send this email and then we'll have breakfast. Maybe then, your stomach will stop growling."

"How did you…"

"Shifter hearing. I'd have thought you were used to that. Especially with your dad being a shifter and all."

"Yeah, I guess. He hasn't exactly been around a lot when it comes to mealtime lately. We all sorta just do our own thing. I'll go out to the kitchen and look around while you write your email. See you when you get finished."

I didn't give Ryker a chance to say anything else. I got up and left. I needed to see what he had in his kitchen before I could figure out what to make him for breakfast. Surely a bear had lots of food in the house, right?

Ryker — 3

I watched my mate flee the office. There really was no other word for it. Troy had given me a little heads up regarding Arin, and what he told me was something I'd pretty much already figured out. My mate was young and inexperienced. It didn't matter to me either way. Actually, my bear loved the thought that our mate hadn't been with anyone else. I once again told him to shut up. It wasn't like we weren't in the same position.

Maybe it would help ease some of our mate's unease if he knew I'd never been with anyone either. Yeah, it was almost unheard of that someone my age hadn't yet been with anyone. But I grew up in a small den where I knew everyone. Knowing none of them were my mate, there just wasn't any desire. It would have been like sleeping with a sibling or cousin. Eww, no.

After quickly typing my email to the regional office letting them know I was taking a week off for family reasons, and that Troy would be the point of contact, I hit send, shut down my computer, and grabbed my phone on my way to the kitchen. That's where my mate was and that's where I wanted to be. I found him with his adorable behind sticking out of the pantry while he was bent down, grabbing something from the bottom shelf. Not a bad view, that's for sure.

"Find everything you're looking for?"

"Wha? Huh?" Arin asked, quickly standing up and spinning around. He had a couple cans of apples in his hands.

"Got a thing for apples, do you? And I asked if you found what you were looking for."

"I did. I was actually just seeing what you had. It appears that you like to eat."

"I do. My bear requires it."

"I understand that. Troy was constantly feeding Elliot when he was pregnant. Elliot said it drove him crazy."

I couldn't help but chuckle at that. Yeah, we were a bit particular when it came to pregnant mates. It didn't seem to matter which species of bear we were either. If our mate was pregnant, our other half was going to almost constantly push us to feed them. Thinking about pregnant mates, I wondered if Arin wanted cubs. Since I was an only child, I wanted as many as I could get. It didn't matter if they were cubs or warlocks, as long as they were healthy and they were with my mate.

Too late, I realized Arin was talking to me. "I'm sorry. What did you say?"

"I asked you if you were ready to eat?" Arin asked as he pointed to the table by the window that was now piled with various breakfast foods. Everything looked and smelled delicious.

"How did I not smell that? It looks amazing. And yes, I'm more than ready to eat. Shall we?" I gestured for Arin to head to the table, and once he was seated, I sat across from him.

"So, would you like to talk some while we eat?"

"Yes. I was too upset to eat yesterday, and I know I need to."

My bear didn't like the idea of our mate not eating. I couldn't quite contain the growl that escaped and Arin froze, his fork halfway to his mouth. "I'm sorry. My bear isn't happy that you skipped dinner yesterday. Please tell me that isn't a regular thing."

"It's not. Normally I love to eat. I was just upset yesterday. I never meant to hurt you. I honestly thought you'd be better off without me. I can't stand the thought of seriously hurting you while we're teleporting, or I'm trying to do something else that I mess up on a regular basis. Papa tracked me down and let me know that even if it wasn't my intention, I'd hurt you. And that just upset me. So much. He really helped me understand how unreasonable and unfair I was being, and he also explained a lot more about what happens when we warlocks find our One. Even if it's when we're so young."

"I've heard that phrase between Troy and Elliot before."

"Yes. You're my One. If you think about it, it makes sense. We all only get one true perfect match. Warlocks simply called that match our One."

"I like that. But back to you not eating, that has to stop. We can't have you skipping meals. My bear doesn't like that."

"Will I get to meet him?"

"Of course. You can meet him whenever you'd like. He'd be more than willing to let you climb all over him at any time. But just so you know, I'm a Kodiak. I'm larger than War but I promise, I'd never hurt you. In either form."

"I know you wouldn't hurt me. But when you say larger than War, how much larger? He's massive and scary as fuck."

I couldn't help but laugh. Our mate was so adorable. I understood completely though. War's bear was rather large, which helped to make him such an intimidating Alpha. But my bear was still bigger. He was grumbling about our mate being scared of him and wanted to meet him even more now.

"I won't lie. My bear is noticeably larger than War's. But you have to know, even War won't hurt you."

"I do. I just don't have anything like that, you know?"

"What are you talking about? You're a badass warlock. You have so many more capabilities than us. Even if you haven't figured everything out yet, you're still powerful. Don't try to deny it. There's something about Edison that isn't normal, and I know you're not quite as powerful as him, but you're no weakling, either."

"I guess."

"Hey. Where is all of this insecurity coming from? From what I've seen, I know it's true. You're badass. You just need to believe it yourself."

"Have you always lived in Alaska? Until you moved here, that is?"

"Don't think I didn't catch what you did. We'll get back to that later. And yes. Until recently, I've always lived in Alaska. I love it on Kodiak Island, but the Alpha up there is an ass. Not quite as bad as the one Troy left behind, but close. I'm seeing a trend, actually. What about you? You're from Amherst. Have you always lived there?"

"How did you know that?"

"Elliot. I don't know him well, but he is mated to my coworker."

"Oh. So, yeah. Arik and I have always lived in Amherst but the others have moved around some."

"Do you miss it?"

"Not really, no. It had its moments. And there's tons to do, but I wouldn't say I'm overly attached to it. I really like it here, and I was happy when War offered to let me stay, even though I wasn't really a member of his den."

"Well, if we do claim each other, you'll become a member if you want. I joined War's den when I moved here. It's not Alaska, but in many ways, Honey Creek is so much better."

"I have no problems with that. I don't like the idea of leaving my brothers. Especially since my dads spend so much time out here with them and their boys. I'm not really close to my two oldest brothers. I mean, they have grandkids older than Arik and me."

"Isn't that unusual?"

"Not for warlocks, no. Especially not for our family."

I nodded at Arin and we finished eating. When I got up to do the dishes, they immediately disappeared from the table. "Alright. That's going to take some getting used to. Where'd they go?"

"I put them in the dishwasher. I can do that for sure. And sometimes I can even wash, dry, and put them away. But not always. I figured it was safer to put them in the dishwasher, and we could run it."

"That works. I'll go start it. Why don't you go into the living room, and we can talk some more?"

"Alright."

After throwing a tab in the dishwasher and hitting start, I turned and headed to the living room in search of my mate. I knew he wasn't there before I even left the kitchen. I followed his heartbeat and his enticing smell and found him back in my bedroom. When I entered, he was standing there in the middle of the room staring at the bed.

"Can I ask you something?"

"Of course. You can always ask me anything, Arin."

"How…are…I'm…"

"Arin, look at me." When he turned those blue eyes my way, I just wanted to wrap him up and never let him go. Somehow, I'd gotten lucky and found my mate. "I'll never hurt you. We can do whatever you want. I'd really like to get to know you. Talking is great for doing that."

"It is. But I was just wondering about later. You know, I just don't know how. I mean… I know how, I just haven't…"

He was adorable. He really was. "I'm aware of that. But don't worry, we can figure it out together. I'm just as clueless as you."

Arin's eye got huge before he was able to reply. "Do you mean that you've never…?"

"Yeah, I hope that's not a problem. I didn't ever smell my mate on my island, and it just didn't appeal to me or my bear to find someone as a replacement. So we became very familiar with, umm, certain other parts of my body that were able to help." I cleared my throat and looked away because after all, it was a bit embarrassing letting my mate know that I'd never had sex before. We were both going to fumble through our first time together, so there was that.

"No, it's okay. It's nice knowing that you're just as inexperienced as I am."

I outright laughed at that. Yeah, I wasn't exactly naïve, and I let him know. "I wouldn't say I'm clueless. I know how things work. And I'm sure when the time strikes, we'll figure things out on our own. Besides, mates have been doing this for a long time. Would you like to meet my bear? Would that help relax you some?"

"Could I?"

"Of course. Come on. Let's head out back and I'll introduce you." I held my hand out for Arin's. Hopefully, he'd take it and let me at least touch him a little. I was getting a little desperate, and my bear was almost constantly pushing me to nudge our mate towards claiming faster. Damn bear. Thankfully, Arin placed his slim hand in mine, and when he did, I felt a tremor go through my body. If Arin noticed, he didn't say anything. I gently pulled my mate through the house and stopped at the table in the kitchen. I let go of his hand and turned to look at him.

"Now remember, he's incredibly large, but I promise, he'd never hurt you."

"I know that. I'm not afraid of you or your bear. I grew up around Dad and he would shift into his tiger as frequently as he could. I know his tiger isn't as big as your bear, but I'm not new to shifters."

"Good. Now, you ready?"

"Yes. I want to meet him. I'm anxious to get to know your other half."

I nodded at my mate and took my clothes off and set them on the chair at the table. "Alright, you're sure?" I asked, reaching for his hand again. He eagerly took it, and I led him to the back yard where I couldn't help myself and I kissed his hand and then let go and walked to the middle of the yard. "He's going to want to smell you and rub all over you. I'll try to make sure he doesn't push you too hard. Even though we haven't claimed each other, he'll know you're our mate and everything should be just fine."

"I'm really not worried. But can I meet him? Please?"

In a blink, I shifted and was standing in front of our mate in my bear form.

"Holy shit. You weren't kidding when you said you were big. You're *huge*! Can you understand me?" I walked up to Arin and he had to look slightly up to me. His forehead was level with my nose. I leaned in and sniffed my mate right where I wanted to put his mating bite. After getting acquainted with his smell, I simply laid down in front of him.

"Hi there. Can I touch you?" I nodded and he squealed with excitement. He started with my round ears. "Wow. They're so soft. But the rest of the hair on you is much coarser. It's still soft and clean feeling, but I love the hair here," he said as he ran his fingers through the hair on my head but quickly went back to my ears. Yep, they were his favorite part it seemed.

After Arin was finished running his fingers through my coat, he climbed on top of me and laid down. "Your bear is beautiful—very intimidating—but I'm not afraid. I can sense that you're still you and that you'd never hurt me. Thank you for showing me your other half. I hope you'll show him to me again, frequently."

All I could do was nod at Arin before I stood up and slowly started walking towards the woods that surrounded the property. He grabbed onto the hair around my neck and hung on. I wasn't planning on going far. Actually, we only went a few feet out of sight of the cabin before I turned around and headed back. There would be plenty of time for Arin to get better acquainted with my bear, but right now, it was time for something else. Maybe I'd get lucky enough to get a kiss from my mate. My bear was happy about that prospect.

Arin — 4

Ryker's bear was massive. He was right; he was noticeably larger than War and Troy. As the Alpha, War's bear was larger than Troy's, but neither of them had anything on Ryker. It didn't matter though, I felt nothing but safe near him. And to get a ride on his back like I'd done so many times with Dad growing up, that was the best part.

All too soon, we were heading back to the cabin. When we arrived back at the deck, Ryker once again laid down, and I slid off of his back and went around and wrapped my arms around my One's furry other half. But when I felt nothing but smooth, warm skin, I realized that Ryker had shifted with ease, and I was now standing in the backyard, hugging my naked One.

"Ryker, I…"

"Arin, please. Just one little kiss? Is that okay? I promise, I'll behave."

I could only nod because my throat closed and there was no way any sound was going to come out of it. Ryker didn't give me any warning before he framed my face with both of his large hands, and then his lips gently covered mine for my first kiss.

Ryker was the absolute best kisser ever. My body felt things it never had before when his lips touched mine. I struggled to keep the moans in and finally just gave up and let one out. When I did, I wished I'd done so sooner. Ryker wrapped his arms tighter around me, but then he was gone. When I looked for him, he was standing there with his back to me, and he went from looking up at the sky to looking out at the woods.

"Ryker?"

"I'm sorry. I didn't mean to get carried away. Why don't you go inside, and I'll be in to get dressed in just a few minutes?" He briefly glanced at me over his shoulder before he strode over to the deck and quickly climbed the stairs that led up to it. When he walked around the side of the cabin, I sighed and went inside. Did I do something wrong? When I saw Ryker's clothes sitting in the chair at the table, I picked them up and just held them. Hopefully, he'd be in to get them from me soon.

Sure enough, he stopped short when he saw me sitting there with his clothes in my arms.

"You okay?" I asked as I hugged his clothing to my chest. They smelled like him and I knew I wanted more of that wonderful scent. Ryker didn't wear cologne. He didn't need to. But he smelled like his body wash, somewhat musky and outdoorsy. He smelled clean and fresh.

"Yeah, I apologize again. I didn't mean to get carried away."

"I wasn't complaining. I enjoyed my first kiss. Can we do it again? I know I'm not that great, but I want to learn."

"Sweetheart, you were perfect. It was my first kiss, too. There's going to be so many firsts between the two of us."

There was no way that Ryker hadn't kissed anyone before. He was so good at it. My shock must have shown, because he smiled at me.

"Can I have my clothes? I'd feel a little more comfortable having this conversation on more even ground."

"Oh, yeah. Here," I replied as I thrust Ryker's jeans and shirt at him. He grabbed them and quickly pulled on his jeans and then his shirt, which was really too bad. I enjoyed looking at all those muscles he had.

"What's going through that mind of yours?"

"Umm…" I ducked my head when I felt my face heat, and I knew it was red. Why did I have to blush so easily? But then again, Arik had been mated to War for almost a year, and he still blushed.

"Never mind. Let's go into the den, and we can sit and talk."

"Alright." I followed Ryker into the den, but instead of sitting on one end of the couch, I sat right in the middle of it. I was really hoping for a repeat of that kiss. It had calmed the vibrations going through my body somewhat, and I wanted to see if it continued to do so. That, and Ryker simply made me feel alive and like I wasn't quite the screw up I felt like I was.

Ryker raised an eyebrow at me before he sat right next to me, only he leaned on the arm of the couch, putting as much room between us as he could. I tried to not be hurt by the move, but in a small way, I was. It seemed that we kept doing that. How did we stop? I quickly scooted to the other end of the couch and looked at my One who had a hurt look on his face.

"Ryker, I simply don't know what to do. I thought maybe sitting in the middle would be better. But then you put as much space between us as possible. What's going on? We're both so unsure at this point; I don't know what to do or how to act."

"You know, for someone so young, you're quite mature. Come here, mate."

I smiled before I crawled towards Ryker. When I stopped beside him, I quickly found myself on my back with my very sexy One on top of me. I looked up into Ryker's eyes as he looked at my mouth and then back up to my eyes. Did he want to kiss me again? I was certainly up for more kissing. So much more kissing. Ryker groaned right before his mouth gently covered mine once more. With a hasty swipe of his tongue across my lips, I knew what he wanted and I quickly opened my mouth and gave him the permission he wanted.

"Just a little more. Oh my fates, Arin. Please? I promise, we'll not go too far, but I need just a little taste of you, sweetheart."

"Yesssss," I said on a moan when he left my mouth and trailed kisses down my chin towards my neck and then down to the juncture where my mate bite from him would go. When he gave it a gentle nip, I felt a flood of fluid release from my hole, and I moaned loudly.

"Fuck!" Ryker said as he sniffed loudly and pulled away. I was left with unfulfilled need, and the vibrations intensified.

"I'm sorry. I'm trying to behave, but it's so difficult when you smell so delicious. I want you, please, don't think I don't. But right now, I need a moment. Okay?"

"Yeah. I'm going to go upstairs and work on some things. I'll be back down later." I quickly teleported myself to the bedroom that Ryker had given me to use, and thankfully, I landed on the bed. Too bad I was in a bed without my One. Things weren't going how I'd hoped, and I honestly didn't know what to do. Maybe Papa could help? Or Elliot. He was a warlock mated to a bear. Right now, I didn't know what to do or where to go.

Remembering the feeling of liquid gushing from my hole, I figured a shower was probably needed before I went in search of some answers, so I got undressed and hurriedly dashed across the hall for the bathroom. I enjoyed a nice, steaming hot shower before I got dressed in clean clothes, and after quickly checking to make sure I was still alone upstairs, I closed the bedroom door and then teleported myself to my dads' cabin on War's property.

The fall this time would have really hurt if not for Papa's help. He stopped me just inches from landing on the stone hearth in their back room.

"Arin? Are you all right?"

"Hi, Papa. I'm fine. But maybe you can release me?" I asked while still suspended just above the fireplace.

"Of course," Papa replied and then I found myself sitting on the couch with him and Dad. "You want to tell us what's going on?" Dad asked. "You're not claimed yet, and we were under the impression that's what you were doing at Ryker's." He was a shifter so maybe he would have a good understanding about what was going on. He was mated to Papa so they were a shifter and warlock, too. That was close enough for me at the moment.

"We're taking our time to get to know each other. But it isn't going well."

"Arin, you know what will happen if Ryker doesn't claim you soon," Papa warned.

"Yes, Papa, I do. But he doesn't know that. He thinks we have plenty of time, and he's in no hurry. We're supposed to be getting to know each other better, but every time we get near each other, things start to escalate and then he stops. The vibrations soften considerably when he's with me and when he's kissing me, but then when he pulls away, they slam back into me. Each time, they get worse."

"You need to let him know. Tonight. Tomorrow is the third day. At some point, you're going to be in so much pain, you won't be able to completely function. He needs to know that you want him to claim you before then. You have to make sure he knows it's your decision, Arin. Otherwise, he might always wonder, and eventually, it could cause problems for you two. Even though you two are fated, that doesn't mean things will always be easy for you.

"How do I get him to stop pulling away? How do I let him know I want to be his?"

Dad and Papa both looked at me and started laughing. Not what I was really going for.

"Arin, you're a warlock. Get rid of his clothes if you can't get him to take them off and then seduce him. Although, if you get rid of his clothes, that would probably do the trick alone. Just make sure you're naked too," Dad told me after he stopped laughing. Surely they weren't serious.

"What? No. I can't do that!"

"Why not?" Papa asked.

"I've never… I'm not sure how to do anything, really. I mean, I know the logistics of everything and how it works, but I'm not Arik. I'm not nearly as bold as him."

"You're right, you're not Arik. But that doesn't mean that's a bad thing. You need to go back to Ryker's, and let him know you want to be claimed," Papa told me. I hung my head and nodded before I found myself falling from the middle of Ryker's kitchen.

"Omph!"

"Arin? Are you okay?"

"Yeah. Nothing new. I can't quite get the hang of the whole reentry thing."

"Where have you been? I went looking for you to see if you wanted some lunch?"

"No, I'm not really hungry. But if you are, I don't mind fixing you something. Just let me know what you want."

"No. I'll wait until you want to eat."

"Please don't. There's no reason for you to wait until I eat. I'm simply just not hungry right now. I've got a lot on my mind."

"Understandable. You going to tell me where you were?"

"I was talking to my dads. What do you say we go for a longer walk in the woods? Would that work?"

"That sounds wonderful. Let me get my pack and we can go."

"What do you need a pack for?"

"To carry supplies."

"But…Yeah, okay." I just shrugged my shoulders and went with it. Hopefully, while we were out, I'd be able to charm my One enough that he'd want me.

Ryker — 5

I was going to go insane if I didn't figure things out with Arin. Fast. My bear was still pissed that I hadn't claimed our mate, and he was becoming more difficult to keep controlled. He wouldn't win, he knew that, but that didn't stop him from trying. The hike in the woods might help. Hopefully, if nothing else, it'd get us out of my cabin, and I could finally breathe something other than Arin's sweet scent.

I thought I'd be okay with just a kiss, but when I got a whiff of his arousal, all I wanted to do was rip his clothes off and claim him. That just wouldn't do. I needed to make sure his claiming was special. It only ever happened once so I couldn't mess it up.

We hiked out to one of my favorite spots that was near my cabin. Arin was a trooper, and no matter how difficult the terrain, he was right there with me. We settled near a grassy knoll that had a natural spring near the bottom of it. It was a perfect spot for a picnic, if only I'd remembered to bring supplies, and it wasn't quite so cold or snowy.

"You look upset. What's wrong?"

I looked at Arin and smiled before answering. "I was just thinking this area would be perfect for a picnic if I'd remembered to bring supplies."

"Oh. I can help with that."

Almost instantly, there was a picnic set up, right next to the spring. The snow was gone, and the little spot Arin had prepared looked warm and inviting.

"Wow. Okay, that really is going to take some getting used to. But that's great! Thanks, Arin."

"No problem. Just let me know if I forgot anything. I've never been on a picnic before so I don't know exactly what I should have brought and what not."

"I'm sure it'll be fine." And it was. Arin had everything we needed for an amazing picnic lunch. I got to know him a little more, and afterward, he showed me some of his magic.

"You're sure it's okay?" He asked looking around.

"Absolutely. I don't smell anyone else anywhere near here. Besides, can't you just stop when you need to?"

"For the most part, yes. Okay, so levitation. I just recently mastered it and it's fun."

Maybe it was fun for him, but before I knew what was happening, I was floating about six feet in the air.

"Okay, so, neat trick. But how do I get down?"

"Oh, that's fairly easy. I just bring you down." I looked at my mate as he smiled at me while I gently floated back to the ground. It was fun but would take time to get completely comfortable with it. Arin showed me how he could make the flowers rapidly sprout and grow and the new leaves fill the trees. He was still working on healings and had difficulties healing something as simple as a paper cut. He was also working on controlling the elements around him, changing the weather type things. And until he could master the majority of what Edison deemed simple mental abilities, he couldn't move on to the more challenging ones. It was a risk, and one he fought me on, but in the end, I talked him into teleporting us back to my place.

"Well, aside from the landing, I'd say you hit the location spot on." I smiled up at my mate who was lying on top of me on my bedroom floor. He blushed at my comment, and I couldn't keep from smiling at him.

"I did warn you. I didn't want to hurt you, and I'm very sorry." Arin tried to climb off of me, but I wasn't having that. My bear and I were both quite content with him on top of us.

"I'm not hurt so I don't see what the issue is."

"Maybe not this time. We were lucky since we landed on the floor. Just wait until we land on something hard and unforgiving. It's happened before."

"I'm willing to take that chance. Arin, about earlier..." I ran my fingers through his short, red hair and smiled up at him. He could leave any time; I just hoped he chose to stay.

"It's okay. I understand. I know this is difficult for you, too. And I'm not meaning to make it harder. I really appreciate how you're so willing to take things slowly. But just so you know, I want to be yours. I'm ready to claim each other when you are."

"Just because I'm okay with taking things slow, that doesn't mean I don't want you. Please know that. I do. More than anything. I just want to be sure this is what you want. You said you were scared, and that's the last thing I want."

"Yes, but not of you. Not really. It's that I'm afraid of causing you pain, either emotional or physical. As you've noticed, we're on your bedroom floor simply because I can't reenter when teleporting. That can get painful. Trust me."

"I do. Which is why I'm willing to wait. I know for a fact that you're worth it. Now, I know we just had a picnic and a hike—" I abruptly stopped when Arin's body started shaking, and he gasped in pain. "Are you alright?"

"Yeah," Arin replied weakly, and then he was gone again. I was left on the floor without my mate in my arms. I could still smell him so I knew he wasn't far, and I located him in the spare room, lying on his bed, curled up in a ball.

"Arin?" I said as I approached him.

"Papa said three days. I had three. It's only been two. Papa. Please."

"Alright. I'll call Troy and get your papa here."

I pulled my phone out of my pocket and quickly called Troy. Thankfully, he picked up right away.

"You're fast if you've already claimed Arin. Elliot and I—"

"I need Edison. Something's wrong with Arin and he's asking for Edison. Only I don't know how to get ahold of him."

"Give me just a few, and I'll have him there."

Before I could hang up and place my phone on the nightstand, Edison was in the room with us.

"How long has he been like this?"

"Just a few minutes. We went for a hike, and he teleported us back here. Then while we were on the floor talking after our landing, he gasped and then he was gone. I found him here."

"This isn't your room? And you still haven't claimed him?"

"No. We were in my room, but he left. This is the spare room. He stayed here last night. What's going on?" Before I could get an answer, Edison and my mate were gone. Dammit. I wish they'd stop doing that. Edison was back before I could even get up off of the bed.

"Ryker, you need to claim your mate. Warlocks usually have three days, but for whatever reason, Arin has only gotten two. He's in a lot of pain because you haven't claimed him yet. It's only going to get worse until you do."

"What? Are you serious?"

"Yes. I promise that I'll tell you all about it later, or Arin will. He should have already said something."

"We've been getting to know each other. Edison, I can't just go claim him."

"Has he said he doesn't accept your claim?"

"Actually, no." Arin had just stated how he was ready just before this happened. Was he trying to tell me something?

"Ryker, Arin needs you. He's your mate, and you need to take care of him," Edison said and then he was gone again. I looked for him in the hallway, but the only thing I heard in the cabin was the sounds or my mate's whimpers coming from my bedroom. Was that where Edison had taken him?

"Arin?"

"Ryker. Please." At my mate's pleas, I couldn't deny him. I wanted him as much as he'd said he did me. I was more than willing to take a chance with his powers not yet fully functioning. I didn't care about that. All I cared about was Arin.

"Let's get these clothes off, shall we?"

When I went to reach for Arin to remove his clothes, we were both suddenly completely naked.

"Okay, *that's* quite useful. I know we were going to wait, but are you sure?"

"Yes. I want to be yours. Claim me, Ryker. Please?"

The growl that came out of my chest made Arin's entire body go flush, and I knew he needed me more than he'd let on. Why didn't he say something sooner? I started with a gentle kiss that Arin readily returned. I moved from his lips to his collarbone and then his nipples. When I sucked on them gently, he gasped and I looked up at him with a feral gleam in my eyes. My bear was very close, and I couldn't wait much longer before he'd completely take over. He was happy I was finally claiming our mate.

"Too much?"

"No, just sensitive. I've never done any of this before. I don't know what to expect."

"How did I get such a treasure?" I asked. "We'll figure everything out together." I moved further down and swallowed Arin's leaking cock in one move.

"Ryker!" he shouted as his body started vibrating harder than ever before. He almost immediately orgasmed and released down my throat. I quickly swallowed everything he gave me, and I smelled more of that enticingly sweet slick that I couldn't wait to get a taste of.

"Mmm, you taste wonderful. Now that we've gotten that one out of the way, let's see what happens when I do this," I said after popping off of Arin's now softening cock and swiftly moving down to his leaking hole. When I started licking-up the slick and thrusting my tongue in and out, his softening cock changed directions and filled again.

"Mpft, Ryker. Please."

Taking that as my cue, before he could realize what was happening, I flipped him over onto his stomach.

"Thank you, Arin for giving us a chance and for coming back. I promise, I'll always cherish everything you give me." I pulled Arin up onto his knees so his back was to my chest. I wrapped my arms around him and held him as I slowly rubbed my cock between his cheeks, spreading his slick everywhere. "So good. Going to love you so much. Forever. I promise, I'll cherish you always." I continued to rub my cock up and down his crack, teasing his hole on every stroke.

"Alpha, please? I need."

"What do you need? Hmm? You ready for me? There's no going back, Arin. If I do this, I'm claiming you and then you're mine for the rest of our lives."

"Yes. Want you. Need you. I'm yours. Forever."

"Yes," I said as I ever so slowly sank my thick cock into his slick hole. It was an intense feeling, and yet, it didn't quite seem like enough just yet. But I knew we'd get there.

"Don't worry, it'll get better, I promise. You feel heavenly, mate. Going to love you, always." I started a slow rhythm of stroking in and out of his body, and in doing so, my body felt like it was on fire.

"Ryker. More. Please."

"Don't worry, you'll get more," I whispered into his ear just before I thrust hard into him. If I didn't have my arms wrapped around Arin, he would have fallen forward on the bed. But that was what he seemed to need because his body started visibly vibrating. I could feel it as much as I could see it. I turned Arin's head for another sweet kiss. When his lips met mine, I never slowed my thrusts that had steadily increased in speed as well as intensity.

When I felt my knot for the very first time, Arin and I both moaned loudly, and he threw his head back onto my shoulder and begged for more.

"Mine, Arin. You're mine, love you," I said just before I thrust hard one last time and stuck inside his tight channel. Within seconds, I felt Arin's channel clamp down on my knot, and he screamed out my name as his cock spurted in front of us. I quickly followed with the most intense orgasm I'd ever experienced, and sunk my fangs into Arin's neck, claiming him as mine. At the same time, I felt a burning sensation on my chest, directly over my heart. I knew it could only be my claiming mark, given to me by Arin.

Something I'd seen many times on Troy's chest. I'd proudly wear Arin's mark for all to see.

I gently laid us down on our sides on the bed, somehow out of the mess we'd made all over it. When my knot went down enough to slip free, I'd get up and clean us up. But for now, I had my precious mate in my arms and my bear and I were both happy and content. We didn't want to go anywhere for the foreseeable future. My cock kept spurting inside Arin, which seemed to keep setting off smaller orgasms for my mate. His channel kept squeezing my knot, which kept up the cycle.

"Thank you, mate," I said as I gently kissed Arin's temple and gave him a tight squeeze.

"Mmm. Sleepy. Hot."

"Rest. I'll be here for you," I said as he drifted off to sleep.

Arin — 6

"Mmm," I sleepily mumbled. When I finally opened my eyes, I found myself staring at Ryker's mate mark, and his strong arms were wrapped around me. I gave the shield a gentle kiss which caused him to moan above me, so I decided to give it another kiss and then a little nibble.

"You keep that up and you'll find yourself stuck on my knot again. Good morning, sweetheart. Are you sure you're ready to be awake?"

"What day is it?" I asked, knowing it wasn't the next day. I'd been warned. When Ryker chuckled, I figured he'd been expecting that question.

"Honestly, I think it's Friday. But it might be Saturday. My phone died a couple days ago, and it wasn't really a priority. I finally got it plugged in last night when your fever broke, and you passed out."

"I'm sorry. I thought I'd have another day to warn you."

"I know you did. And I appreciate it. I did manage to sneak to the kitchen and raid the pantry several times while you were…"

"In the midst of my first ever fertile cycle? Yes. I promise, it'll never be that intense again."

"That's too bad. I wasn't complaining at all. I rather enjoyed all of the levitating and teleporting."

"What?" I shrieked and looked up at Ryker's face and discovered that he was quite serious and looked exhausted.

"Let's see if this works," Ryker said just before he sent me his memories of the past several days. It started with Papa showing up and then Ryker claiming me in the most sweet and romantic way. I had indeed levitated us on more than one occasion while Ryker was knotted inside me. And at other times, I'd teleported us in the midst of it. One thing I did notice, in his memories, we'd only fallen from the middle of the room a few times. He'd always put himself on the bottom somehow to take the impact. My One was so very sweet and thoughtful. But for the most part, we usually just teleported from the bed to another surface in the house.

"Really? We didn't crash land every time?"

"So it worked? You can communicate with me through a bond like shifters do? I wasn't sure it would. I've only gotten little glimpses of you over the past several days, as well as other things."

I gasped and hoped he meant that he'd detected the heartbeat. It was there, strong as could be. There was only one, so that meant we were having a single cub or warlock. I hoped that wasn't a disappointment.

"You could never be a disappointment to me, sweetheart. And neither will our child. I heard the heartbeat, yes, but I've been very focused on you."

"How did you? Are you reading my mind?"

"I don't have to, Arin. Right now, you've got your mind completely open to me. Mine is the same, if you'd just look."

So I did. I immediately felt the love that he had for me and our unborn baby. His bear was there, in the background, and he too was delighted about the mate and child. "Wow. Your bear is happy."

"Yeah, he is. He wants to see you again, soon, but right now, what do you say about a shower and some fresh sheets and then some lunch?"

"That all sounds wonderful. If I can smell us, I'm sure we stink to you."

"We could certainly use a trip through the shower, that's for sure."

"Ryker?"

"Yeah, sweetheart?"

"I just want to say thank you for everything. I know this didn't all happen how either of us intended, but I promise I'll be the best mate I can. I know I'm going to fumble, but please don't give up."

"Oh, sweetheart, I'll never give up on you. Or us. We're in this together, and I'm so very proud to have you for my mate. Now, let's shower and then we'll get some lunch. My bear is pissed that we're talking instead of eating. You're pregnant and he's demanding that I feed you."

"Food does sound wonderful. I'm starving!" I said before I somehow managed to teleport us to the bathroom and into the shower with only a small mishap. Ryker's cabin had a nice-sized master bathroom, and for that, I was thankful. I was also grateful that I was able to safely teleport us to the bathroom without a complete crash landing.

"That really is handy," Ryker said as he turned on the water, and we were immediately covered in ice-cold water.

"What the!" I gasped before I was able to get out of the spray.

"Sorry. I didn't think it'd be this cold. But we haven't showered in a while."

"It's okay," I replied as I adjusted the temperature and stood back in the soothing spray. "Mmm. This feels so good." When I opened my eyes, I noticed that Ryker's tired eyes were once again on me.

"Yeah, I'm tired, but it's not anything a good nap won't help."

"Okay, that's a little unnerving."

"You just need to close your thoughts to me. But please, don't completely shut me out of our bond."

"No, I'd never do that. I want you to be there. I just need to get used to it."

"You don't have to remain completely open. But know that I have absolutely nothing that you can't see. *Things just take time to figure out. Like the mate mark you gave me. It's beautiful. Now that it's stopped itching, it's got an almost vibration feeling to it. Is that normal? It's amazing and I love the fact that you marked me. My bear and I are both proud to wear your mark, Arin.*"

Having Ryker communicate the second half to me in our bond was wonderful, and helped me understand more on how to curb what was projected to him and what wasn't.

"*I'm glad you like your mark. I wasn't exactly sure how large you'd want it so I didn't make it as big as Troy's. Anyway, shouldn't we be showering?*"

"I just figured you were enjoying the water. But yes, we should. I need to feed you."

We quickly showered, and then after, I dried us off and dressed us in clean clothing. I looked longingly towards the bed as I also changed the sheets. I'd love a nap.

"Hey, Ryker? After we eat, we can take a nap, right?"

"Yeah. That sounds heavenly. But first I need to get you fed. Come on." We left the bedroom in search of food that was more substantial than sandwiches or protein bars. Ryker's bear wasn't a fan of those I'd realized as I heard his beast grumble about real food.

"Alright, what would you like? You pretty much filled the pantry before we claimed each other, but we didn't eat anything that had to be cooked so..." Ryker stopped mid-thought when he got a whiff of the steak and all the trimmings I'd cooked. I was hungry and ready for some real food.

I was sitting at the small table in the kitchen window with two thick, juicy steaks on plates in front of me.

"Yeah, that works," Ryker said before joining me. He seemed happy, and I was grateful that he didn't complain about not cooking.

"I made yours medium. I figured that would do?"

"Medium works. I get to fix supper though, alright?"

"Sure. That sounds nice. Thank you for taking such good care of me over the past several days."

"I'll always take care of you, sweetheart. You're my mate."

"I appreciate it, all the same. And I'm sorry I didn't give you a better warning about what to expect."

"I knew some. Troy had mentioned little bits of things every so often. Nothing in detail, but a few small things here and there."

"Do you need to get to work soon?"

"No. Not today at least. I'll call Troy later after our nap and check in. But remember, he's mated to your brother. He knew exactly what to expect."

"I guess that helps."

"It does. Now, eat up so we can get to that nap. I'm looking forward to holding you in my arms again. And maybe this evening after dinner, you'd like to meet my bear again?"

"I'd love to. Can I have a ride again? I know that's probably not a proper thing to ask, but I have such fond memories of riding on Dad when I was a small child. Papa would laugh at us but wouldn't pull me off. So many times I wished I was a shifter instead of a warlock. But then I came into my powers, and now I wouldn't trade being a warlock for anything. It can be really amazing, what I can do, but yet Arik can't. But he's always had me, and I may have fumbled along the way, but we always got there and had fun."

"I'm glad you had a good childhood. Mine was drastically different."

"Yes, I saw through our bond. I'm so sorry, Ryker."

"It's okay. Things worked out exactly as the fates wanted them to. And we're together so that's all that matters."

"Do you think your old den will come looking for you?"

"I hope not. If they do, I'm afraid of what might happen now that I'm part of War's den. It wouldn't be just bears they'd be dealing with. I don't think they'd know what hit them. Your papa scares me."

"It's so funny you say that. Troy said the same thing. But that all changed when Elliot was pregnant with the triplets."

"Yes, I remember him telling me that story. I still haven't had that moment with your parents. Hopefully, I get there soon because right now, they really are intimidating."

We continued eating and talked about small things here and there. Ryker seemed happy and that made me feel like we'd finally done something right. By the time I was just a little over halfway finished with my steak, I started to lose steam and couldn't stifle the yawns from coming out.

"Sweetheart, come on. Let's go upstairs and take that nap. You're beat."

"I'm sorry. I didn't mean to get so sleepy all of a sudden."

"It's understandable. You've been through a lot over the past several days. You need food and rest. You've had the food, now comes the nap." Just as I was about to attempt to teleport us to the bedroom, Ryker picked me up and carried me upstairs in his arms. I discovered that I rather enjoyed being in his arms and snuggled into the crook of his neck.

"I like this."

"I do too. I'll have to sit you down so I can pull the covers back, but I'm looking forward to snuggling up with you and resting. Don't tell anyone, but I'm tired too."

"I'm sure you are. Not only did you have to deal with me this week, but you took care of me."

"Trust me, it was no hardship. And you say it'll never be like that again?"

"Yes and no. It won't ever be that intense again. But it will be more than what shifters go through when they have a heat cycle."

"Mmm, I'm looking forward to it," he told me as he gently set me down in the middle of the bed, after I'd turned the blankets back. "Thanks for the help with the blankets."

"That was nothing. Now you're going to join me, right?"

"Absolutely. Do you need to use the bathroom? I probably should have asked before I put you in bed."

"No, I'm good. But you're more than welcome to if you need to."

"Nope." Ryker said as he crawled onto the bed and covered us both up. By the time he was lying on his back, I was ready to snuggle up and was instantly in his arms. "Sweet dreams, sweetheart." Ryker said just as I dozed off.

Ryker — 7

My mate was absolutely adorable. Everything about him was. I even found his quiet snores cute. With him in my arms, I realized that it was easy to quickly doze off. When I woke again, it was to a still-sleeping mate curled up in my arms. The fates were so kind to me.

My bladder was screaming at me though, so I gently maneuvered out from his grasp. How I managed, I don't know, but my bladder thanked me when I made it to the bathroom. Checking on Arin through our bond, I discovered he was still in a deep sleep, and since it would probably be a while yet before he was awake, I quietly grabbed my phone from the nightstand and went downstairs into the small room I used as a home office.

I sat down at the desk and powered on my laptop, and when I did, I realized it was in fact Monday. "Well, there went that week. And now I'm talking to myself." I shook my head and logged into the company web portal and checked my email and immediately closed it. Yeah, those could wait since there were so many.

Picking up my cellphone, I decided to give Troy a call and let him know we were still alive. He answered on the first ring.

"Well, look who finally got out of bed." I groaned at Troy's comments and knew I was probably in for a ration of shit.

"You know I didn't even have to give you a call. I can just go back upstairs and curl back up with my sleeping mate."

"No. Don't. Elliot has been asking if I've heard from you yet. After your last call, he's been a little worried."

"I haven't had a chance to talk to Arin about that too much, yet. But I will say this, Arin's fertile period, as he calls it, didn't end until just this morning."

"Wow. That was a couple days longer than Elliot's. You doing okay?"

"Yeah, we're both fine. Thanks for asking. Tired. And sore in all kinds of places."

"Yep, been there, too. Congratulations on your mating though. And since Edison said it was pretty much a guarantee, congrats on your little cub or warlock. Or cubs or warlocks. Damn, you know what I mean."

I couldn't stop laughing. He was trying his best, but it was still funny. "I knew what you meant. And thanks. Arin said there is one but hasn't said if it's a cub or warlock yet. Will he know already?"

"Yeah, he should. Unless he just got pregnant in the last day or so, then it'll probably take him a couple more days. Edison would have more input and answers."

"Yeah, I think I'll hold off on that. He was pretty intense the last time I saw him."

"He's not so bad. And they love their boys—all five of them—but they're closer to the twins then the others."

"Good to know. I promise, I'll bring Arin over tomorrow. But he's worn out, and I promised him he could see my bear again this evening. My bear is grumbling about not having seen our mate in the past several days, and Arin seems anxious to see him again."

"Elliot loves my bear as much as he loves me. I'm sure things will be just fine."

"I'm not worried. He did great the first time I introduced them. And he was telling me about how when he was younger, he used to go around riding on Wallace's back."

"No way. Really? I'm still waiting for the triplets to be old enough to do that."

"Troy, they're seven weeks old. You're going to be waiting years."

"Hush. Don't rain on my parade. I'm hoping and waiting."

I laughed again, I simply couldn't help myself. "Alright. Arin is starting to stir up in bed. I'll see you tomorrow."

"Sounds good. Enjoy your last quiet evening." I didn't quite catch what he said in time to ask him about it. But I'd be sure to ask tomorrow. Right now, I had a mate that was waking up, and I needed to be sure I was there for him so I ran upstairs, and he was just rolling over as I entered the bedroom.

"Good evening. Did you enjoy your nap?" I asked as I sat down on the edge of the bed. Looking at my mate, I thought again how lucky I was. His red hair, blue eyes, and slim build were deceiving though. There was nothing delicate about my sweetheart. No, he was a force to be reckoned with, if only he could get past his own insecurities.

"I'm good. Have you been up long?"

"No. I went to the office to check my email and decided to ignore it until later in the week. I also called Troy. He mentioned something about Elliot being worried. We really should eventually talk about everything that's happened over the past week. Specifically, the vibrations that you were experiencing. For now, it'll keep. But I want to talk about it, today."

"You sure? I'm more than willing to talk about them now."

"I'm still processing, but right now, what sticks out the most is the vibrations became painful. What does that mean exactly? You're not in any pain now, are you?"

"Not really, no. It comes and goes. They're more a gentle hum now. It's directly linked to the feeling you experience through your mate mark. As you know, we have our One. And how that works is, we sense everything around us through their aura. The feeling from this is like a gentle hum or vibration going through our bodies. When we get close to our One, those vibrations intensify. Once we're claimed, the vibrations mellow out and aren't quite as gentle as we felt before claiming but aren't as intense either. If we're not claimed, the vibrations will continue to intensify until it becomes too painful to function. Once claimed, the only time they intensify is when I'm either pregnant or going through my fertile cycle. As a warlock, I'll only have one a year. And until I met you, I never had one so I wasn't expecting how intense it was. Elliot took Troy away for five days when they claimed each other. And from what I'm told, he more than earned his nickname."

"Okay, that's even more to process. So you were just going to let yourself be in pain? That doesn't make sense. Not when I could help." Not only was I upset, my bear was as well.

"I thought I was doing the right thing. You've seen over the past several days how clumsy I can be. And we were getting to know each other."

"Okay, let's just get this out there right now. I don't need to be saved from you. I'm not fragile. I know you're not ready to believe in yourself yet, but you'll get there. I already believe in you, and I know that you would *never* hurt me. Not seriously. You might drop me on my behind but that's okay. I'm more than willing to have a sore ass. You're worth that and so much more. If only you'd see that."

Arin nodded, and I was willing to let it slide for now. But we were certainly not finished with that topic yet.

"So how about dinner, and then we'll go outside for you to see my bear again? You head to the bathroom, and I'll go down to the kitchen and start supper. Anything in particular you're in the mood for?"

"Anything you want. I'm not a picky eater."

"Alright. I'll see you downstairs in a few. I'll go see what I can find while you take care of business up here. And you might want to give your brother a call. Or maybe Edison."

"Nah, Papa knows I'm okay. He can't ever be completely shut off."

"Do I even want to know?"

"It's not as creepy as it sounded. He's not listening or peeping."

"Okay then. That's just…I don't know if I want to know exactly."

"Don't worry about it. You go find supper, and I'll go to the bathroom and then be down."

"Alright. See you in a few." I gave Arin a quick kiss before I got up and left the bedroom as he walked to the bathroom. I could find something for dinner, right?

I sure could. After a delicious dinner of grilled chicken, vegetables, and fresh fruit, I was ready for Arin to meet my bear again. He was happy that I'd finally claimed Arin as ours, and he was more than anxious to sniff around our pregnant mate.

"Because you're pregnant, my bear wants to sniff around you for a few. Please don't be alarmed."

Arin giggled, and it was so adorable I couldn't help but smile at him.

"I'm not worried. Your bear could never really scare me. But come on, get naked so I can give him a kiss."

"Not exactly how I wanted you to tell me to get naked but okay, I guess." I started removing my clothes, but before I could shift, Arin was in my arms and then his lips were on mine, giving me gentle, quick pecks.

"I want to kiss you, too. And hopefully, later, you'll get naked with me upstairs?"

"Sweetheart, I'm always willing to get naked with you. Just let me know when and where." I got another sweet smile from my mate, and then he pulled out of my arms, and I quickly shifted. My bear was excited about the baby our mate was carrying, and after a few quick sniffs, I laid down so Arin could climb on my back. After he was secure and ready, I took off for a long walk, deep in the woods. About thirty minutes from the cabin, I made a concerning discovery though.

"Sweetheart, I don't suppose you could teleport us back to the cabin, could you?"

"I'd feel better about it if you shifted first. Why? What's up?"

I laid down, still fully on alert of the surrounding forest, but when Arin slid off of my back, I quickly took my human self.

"The cabin, quick," I told him as I wrapped my arms around him. Immediately, we were back in the yard where I'd left my clothes, and I grabbed them and quickly dressed.

"Okay, so would you be willing to teleport us to War's place? I could drive us if you aren't."

"I don't mind teleporting us. But you want to tell me what's going on?"

"I smelled a bunch of bears that don't belong. Every one of them smelled like arctic bears, so they're either polar bears or Kodiaks, or both. As far as I know, I'm the only Kodiak, and there are only a few polar bears other than Troy. I've met Ivan, Sam, and their two kids. These didn't smell like them."

"Why do I have a feeling that's a bad thing? The fact that you smelled other bears, that is."

"Only because it is," I said as I quickly put on my boots and bent down to lace them up and tie them "We need to get our phones, lock up the cabin, and get to War's."

In a blink, I had all those things, and we were instantly at War's house. I stopped short when the scenery changed. No longer were we at the base of the stairs at our cabin. We were in the middle of War's kitchen and were surrounded by Arin's brothers and their mate and One.

"Where's Papa and Dad?"

"They went to Amherst for a couple days to discuss some things with Arthur and Patrick. Why?" Elliot asked.

"That would explain why they didn't tell anyone. We were out for a stroll in the woods by my cabin, and I smelled several other shifters. All bears, and all new. They aren't any I've scented before. But they're either polar bears or Kodiaks. I thought you should probably know," I told War. He looked thoughtful for a moment and then looked over to Troy and then back at me.

"You expecting company?" War asked me.

"I didn't think so. My old Alpha was an asshole, but he wasn't overly upset when I left. It's been a couple days since they went through. My bear didn't hear or detect them when they did, but that's not surprising. I was otherwise occupied, and I detected the scents a fair distance from our place."

"Understandable. But I wouldn't be surprised to have my old Alpha show up and try to cause problems, I'd say it's probably him. Especially after everything Ivan said they went through with him and the elders up there," Troy said.

"We'll try to figure it out if we can. Troy, get ahold of the rest of the den and call a meeting. We need to make sure we aren't taken by surprise. Especially after what happened to Ivan and his group," War said, but was cut off by the appearance of Edison and Wallace.

"You won't need to call. I can tell you what you need to know," Papa said as he looked around the room. When he opened his arms for Arin, he left my side and went to his carrier and gave him a tight hug. "Congratulations on your claiming. Now, do you two want to know what you're having? I've already goofed before; I want to make sure I don't do it again."

Arin — 8

"Arin said there was only one, and as long as it's healthy, I don't care what we're having. But if Arin wants to know, that's fine." Ryker said as he walked up behind me.

"Congratulations to you too, Ryker. And welcome to the family. I have something for you. Arin will always be able to get a location and communicate with you through your bond, but I won't. Here's your amulet. It allows me to locate you, always. As well as a few other things," Papa told Ryker while holding out the beautiful blue stone. He took it and immediately put it on.

"Thanks, Edison. I'll be sure to always keep it on."

"Yes, that would be wise. To answer your question with regards to who is lurking in the woods, it's nobody good. Troy, son, what's left of your den, as well as the others that attacked Ivan's, have come because they decided the ones that escaped them need to be dealt with."

"You're saying my old Alpha is here," Troy asked.

"Yes. As are all of his supporters. For now, they're camping much deeper in the woods. I can find out what their plans are, and with where they're located, they won't be able to get here in under a day's time."

"Are Arin and our baby in danger?"

"Everyone in that group is here for malicious intent. But no. Arin isn't in any danger. And neither is your baby. I will never let anything happen to any of you. I'll go and put a spell on your place and the immediate woods surrounding it. It'll keep those who wish harm away. They won't be able to enter the yard. And no matter what, I'll always be monitoring your place until the threat is dealt with."

"Thank you. My first priority is obviously Arin. I don't want anything to happen to him, and I know I won't always be able to be with him."

"It's not like I'm completely helpless, you know," Arin scoffed.

"I know that, sweetheart. But I can't help it. I'm going to worry. So is my bear. It's just in our nature. Elliot is a warlock, but I'm sure Troy is the same way and I know War is."

I looked at my brothers' other halves and sure enough, they were silently nodding.

"At first, I wanted to suggest that you bring Arin here and stay until this all blows over, but thinking about it, I know it'll be better with you there. You can keep an eye and nose out for us," War said while looking at us.

"I will. You know it." Ryker looked at War and then at me. I gave him a tight hug and when he kissed my temple, my heart melted.

"Ryker, thank you."

"For what, sweetheart?"

"For everything. For being you and wanting me."

"Always. No matter what."

I stayed in Ryker's arms, happy and content. I smiled up at my One. He really was easy on the eyes. Why did I ever run?

"Not now, sweetheart. It's alright. We're together just as the fates wanted us to be. We'll get through all of this. I promise."

"How?"

"You're completely open to me at the moment. Not that I mind. I like knowing your thoughts. Especially when you think I'm nice to look at."

I couldn't help it, I snorted and looked at him.

"Alright you two. The mate bond is wonderful, but we need to get things figured out," War interrupted us, and I couldn't help but roll my eyes at him. I really liked my twins' mate even if he was in serious Alpha mode.

"Sorry, Alpha," Ryker said to War, who then rolled his eyes at Ryker.

"Yeah, well, you're family now, and even if you weren't, I'd still worry. Elliot, I'm afraid to say that we're probably going to need to ask Ivan and Sam to move into one of the cabins here. They live the furthest away, and they were a direct target once and still probably are. Since they don't have the added benefit of one of them being a warlock, I'd really feel better with them closer."

"That's okay. I completely understand and have no problems with either of them," Elliot told our brother-in-law and snuggled up to Troy.

"Great. Edison, if I could talk to you for a few minutes in the office, I'd appreciate it. Everyone else, please go home and rest. I'm sure we're all going to need it eventually, so why not start now?"

"He's right. Get some rest and know that everyone is safe. There won't be any issues for some time yet. I promise," Papa said to our group and we all nodded as he walked off to War's office.

"Ryker. Again, welcome to the family. Why don't you take Arin back home and get some more rest? I'm sure that after the week you two have had, you could use some more sleep. And if your bear is anything like mine, he's going to be pushing you to pamper your pregnant mate," War said to my One with a smile. I remember when Arik was pregnant with the twins. War had a fit any time Arik tried to do anything. He kept blaming his bear, but I secretly thought it was just an excuse to dote on his mate.

"Dad?"

"Don't worry, Arin. You know your papa won't let anything happen to any of you. But you also know he can't just go and eliminate them."

"Yeah, I do. Thanks for coming back. Everything okay in Amherst?"

"Yeah, everything's fine. You two head to your place and get some rest. It may have been a while, but I remember what those first few days were like after Edison would go through a fertile cycle. Go rest. And Ryker, welcome to the family, son." Dad gave Ryker a pat on the shoulder and then walked off towards the direction Papa had gone with Troy. War followed him, and that left me with my brothers and my One.

"I have to go feed the twins. We'll see you in the morning?" Arik asked, looking between the two of us.

"Yes. But do you need any help?"

"No, I have it. And I'm sure Dad will find his way upstairs in just a few minutes to help anyway."

"True. Thanks, Arik."

"What for?"

"Everything," I replied before I looked at Ryker, and then poofed us to the cabin that was first Ryker's, but was now ours. I loved it already and couldn't wait to raise our family there. Unfortunately, the landing left a little to be desired.

"You know, I should have been expecting it, but I just never know. You're really good at this. And so far, you've only had us crash land just a few times. Already, you're improving. You said you used to never be able to have a reentry go smoothly," Ryker said as I laid on top of him. We were in the bedroom, but I'd missed the bed. Even though we were on the floor, Ryker didn't seem in any hurry to let me up. He just tightened his arms around me more.

"I guess I haven't thought about that. You're right though. I wonder if you claiming me has anything to do with it."

"Maybe. Or maybe you've just gained more confidence in yourself. I'm not sure what the real issue was to begin with, but I know that you're doing well now. I'm so proud of you. And I always will be."

I couldn't stop myself from yawning, and when I looked down at Ryker, he gazed up at me with a smile on his face.

"I love you, Arin. Why don't we get some sleep? It's been an eventful and tiring week."

"Love you, too," I replied and yawned again.

"Come on, let's get you to bed. You're exhausted."

"I'm sorry, Ryker. It just hit me all of a sudden."

"No need to apologize. You're just worn out. Let's brush our teeth and then I'll tuck you in."

"Are you not joining me?" I asked as I got up off of my One and stood up.

"I will after I check the cabin. My bear simply requires it. Sorry. I won't be but a few more minutes."

"Okay," I said as we walked into the bathroom to take care of our nighttime routine. After that was accomplished, I removed my clothes, with a little *help*, and then crawled into the bed, naked as could be.

"I must admit, I appreciate your choice of bedtime attire. I'll be back in just a few minutes, sweetheart," Ryker said as he pulled the blankets up and gave me a gentle kiss. I sighed and smiled at him. The bed smelled like us, but it was Ryker's scent in it that relaxed me. I really did have a sexy One. The fates had been kind to me.

Waking up snuggled in Ryker's arms was something I looked forward to for the rest of our lives. Unfortunately, we had to get up. Ryker had already missed a week of work and needed to get back to his old routine. I would go hang out with Papa, and hopefully, we could work on some of my powers that I was still trying to master.

"Good morning, sweetheart. Did you sleep well?" Ryker asked from above me. I gave his mate mark a quick kiss before I answered, but when I did, he moaned loudly and I felt his hard cock twitch between us.

"I did. But now I'm distracted from getting up, and I think I want to do that again."

Ryker groaned and flopped onto his back and let me do whatever I wanted to his body. We were finally able to leave our bed an hour later. After a quick shower, we were downstairs and getting ready for the day.

"I'm late. I won't have time for breakfast," Ryker said, but I stopped him with a hand on his chest. I felt guilty because it was my fault he was running late.

"I'm sorry, Ryker. I promise to behave from now on."

"What are you talking about? Hang on," Ryker said as he reached into his pocket and grabbed his phone.

"Hey, Troy. I'm going to be about another hour, okay? Great. See you then."

"Alright. Now that's taken care of, come here." Ryker grabbed my hand and gently pulled me over to the table by the window. When he sat down on one of the chairs, he pulled me down onto his lap. "Arin, please don't ever apologize for what happened this morning. I enjoyed everything you did, and in case you didn't realize it, my knot stuck in you should have given that away."

I couldn't help but blush at the thought. But he was right. His knot didn't seem to want to go down this morning, which is why he was now late for work.

"I wasn't apologizing for what we did, only that it caused you to be late."

"I didn't stop you, and I never will. Thankfully, I work with other shifters, and they know that mates always come first. Troy has been late many times and still works shorter hours so he can get home to Elliot and their triplets. Jai, although he hasn't yet found his mate, I know he completely understands."

"Alright. Now, how about a quick breakfast? That way you can get to work and not need the entire hour like you told Troy?"

"That sounds wonderful," Ryker said before he gave me a quick kiss. I climbed off his lap, and when I moved out of the way, the table was loaded with all of Ryker's favorite breakfast foods. We dug in, and when he kissed me goodbye at his truck and took off for work, I teleported to Dad and Papa's cabin. Ryker was working, so I needed to do the same, right?

"Good morning, Arin. Come on in. Edison is in the kitchen cleaning up."

"Good morning, Dad," I replied as I gave my sire a quick hug. I loved my family and was so thankful for them. Now I also had Ryker and a little one on the way. Could life get any better?

"Morning, Arin. I've been expecting you. You ready to get started?"

"Yes, Papa. I'm ready. I don't want to disappoint my One. He's told me so many times how proud he is of me, but I can't help but feel like I could do so much better."

"Son, you should listen to your One. You have nothing to be ashamed of. You're still very young. And although it's almost unheard of for a warlock to find their One so young, you have. Ryker is only going to add to your strength. Be sure to remember that."

"I will, Papa." That was something to think about, and it made sense. Since Ryker had claimed me, I had noticed an increase in the energy that was coursing through my body. Tasks were easier, and certain forms of magic I'd previously always messed up, were now only wonky some of the time. Like when I teleported over here. My reentry was perfect. I landed on my feet, exactly where I intended. Hmm.

"I see you're realizing a few things. That's good. Now, let's begin."

I looked at Papa and smiled before I went to work concentrating on what he was teaching me.

Ryker — 9

It was no use. I couldn't concentrate. I'd only been mated for not quite a week, and it was no use. My bear wasn't quite ready to leave our mate and come to work.

"I recognize that look. Tell me why you're even here? I've been there, and I know how difficult it is to come to work right after you've mated. And you two have only been mated for five days. Take some more time. I did."

"I know. But I'm the boss, and there are certain things I'm required to do."

"True. Okay, so why didn't you bring Arin with you? He's not super pregnant yet, and he's fun to be around. I love him, and it's always fun to watch him try to do magic."

I couldn't contain my growl. My bear and I didn't like that last part. Bringing Arin to work with us, we were both all for that. But Troy's comment about Arin and magic, rubbed me a little wrong.

"Hey now, what'd I do?" Troy asked, holding up both his palms.

"Ryker? You okay? I'm getting feelings of anger from you through our bond?"

"I'm fine, sweetheart. I'm sorry. I'll be better about that. Troy just said something that pissed me off. Let me get rid of him, and I'll be right with you."

"'kay"

I looked up at Troy and did my best to not rip his head off. "I'd appreciate it if you and everyone else in the family would be a little more considerate when discussing Arin and his powers. He's incredibly young and it's my understanding that it isn't uncommon for warlocks to spend the first fifty to a hundred years mastering their gifts. The constant teasing he's subjected to from his brothers is doing nothing but causing self-confidence issues and hindering his progress."

"I honestly meant nothing by it, Ryker. I'll talk to Elliot and make sure he talks to his brothers. We won't say another thing about it. Promise."

Troy got up and couldn't leave my office fast enough. And that made me feel like a complete ass. He was my brother-in-law, and I should be nicer to him. Especially since he'd been so wonderful and covered for me last week. I banged my forehead on the desk, and then I felt my mate run his finger through my hair at the same time I smelled his sweet scent.

"Ryker, what's wrong, love?"

"I just chewed Troy's ass out for something that technically wasn't his doing. Come here, I need some cuddles," I said as I scooted back and pulled Arin down onto my lap and wrapped him up in my arms. I buried my face in his neck and gave his mating bite a gentle kiss, and when he moaned I knew I needed to stop or we'd end up in a compromising position here in my office. "Sorry. I'll behave."

"Hmm, you got mad when I said those exact same words this morning. I like it when you misbehave. Please do."

I chuckled at my precious mate. He was just too cute. "As much as I'd love nothing more than to get into trouble with you, I can't. I'm behind on some paperwork, and I have to get it finished before I can head home. But you're more than welcome to hang out if you want. Troy is probably out at his desk, sulking. Jai is out at the lake checking on something, but he'll be back soon."

"Troy probably isn't sulking. Elliot came with me so I'm sure they're doing pretty much the same thing you and I are." Arin ran his fingers down my chest, and I couldn't help but catch the innuendo. I gave in, because in the end, I knew I wouldn't get anything accomplished until I did.

After I had Arin screaming my name into my hand as I sucked down his release, he passed out for a much-needed nap. I carried him over to the couch that was in the office, and after I righted his clothing, I covered him with the blanket that was thrown over the back. Once my body was back under control, I went out to the main room in search of a bottle of water.

"Hey Ryker. Where's Arin?" Elliot asked as I approached Troy's desk. Troy on the other hand, was nowhere to be found.

"He's taking a nap on the couch in the office. He's still a little worn out from last week."

"Yeah, I think it took me about three or four days to really recover from when Troy claimed me. It's brutal and seems a little unfair at times."

"I'm not complaining, but I'd have to agree. I didn't realize he'd tire so easily, nor did I realize it would last so long. Heat cycles for shifters end when they conceive."

"It's the same with warlocks, but it'll only last up to a week's time. So it won't ever go beyond that. The average time seems to be three days for established couples. Next time shouldn't be nearly as long, or intense," Elliot smiled at me as he looked at me with understanding.

"That's good to know. I'm worried about him. Should he be this tired?"

"Creating a new life can be especially tiring on carriers. Oh my fates! He's having a warlock! That's why he's extra tired!" Elliot screeched.

"What? He's what?" I asked, confused.

Just then, Edison appeared. That was cool but was going to take longer than a week to get used to.

"Yes, your brother is having a warlock, but will be just fine. So will his little warlock. He's having just the one, and he'll eventually end up being quite a handful, but a treasure. I'm sorry if you didn't want to know, Ryker. Arin was going to be able to tell in another day or two." Edison turned and glared at Elliot who actually looked embarrassed.

"Sorry. I wasn't thinking," Elliot said, apologizing.

"No, it's okay. I honestly have no preference at all. I'm going to love our children no matter what. But why is he extra tired just because he's carrying a warlock?"

"Because his body is going to unconsciously be overly protective of it. All children are a blessing, but warlock children seem to be more difficult to carry. Which might be part of the reason why most warlocks don't have but one or two children. Wallace and I are an exception. My family line being the main reason for that; it helps that he's also a shifter."

"Yeah, but you two only have one child that's a shifter," I stated, still somewhat confused.

"True, but that doesn't mean we weren't willing. And it wasn't that we needed a child such as Arik. We just happened to be very much in love and wanted more than one child." Edison looked fondly while thinking of his One. My mate's parents were an ideal fated pair. They were very much in love, which was how fated pairings worked. Once you found your fated One that was it. You were completely devoted to them for the rest of your lives. I was never more thankful that I'd finally found my mate. Arin was a true blessing, and I'd never forget that.

"I wanted to talk more about what you mentioned last night, if you had the time," I said to my mate's father.

"Sure. Although, I honestly don't have any more information for you yet. War was asking pretty much the same thing this morning. They've camped quite a distance away, and as of yet, I'm unsure of their exact plan."

"Okay. I'm sorry. I don't mean to push. Edison, can I ask you something?"

"Of course, you can. You're always welcome to ask anything, Ryker."

"I don't understand why everyone is always mentioning how clumsy Arin is? I didn't mean to, but I chewed Troy out for it just a little while ago."

"You're mated to my brother. He's teleported you more than once, right?" Elliot asked, but I just looked at him with a blank look.

"*Ryker?*"

"I'm just outside the office, sweetheart. I'll be there in just a few. I'm having a discussion with your Papa and brother at the moment."

"No, I'll come to you. Give me just a minute to wake up a little more."

"Okay. See you soon."

"Yes, I'm mated to your brother. Yes, he's teleported us more than once. Several times actually. Sometimes we fall, others we don't."

"Really? Huh. I wonder what happened that he all of a sudden doesn't mess it up every time."

"There's a reason why all of a sudden Arin isn't struggling nearly as much as he used to, Elliot. He's found his One, and Ryker is very important to him," Edison told Elliot who looked over at me.

"I can tell you what's happened. He's receiving the unconditional support and encouragement he needs. You may not realize it, but the picking hurts. And it only adds to his stress, which causes more mishaps," I glared at Elliot who looked over my shoulder, and when I turned, there was Troy striding towards his mate. Suddenly, Arin appeared beside me, and I looked lovingly at my mate. He was so beautiful.

"Hello, sweetheart. Did you sleep well?"

"I did. I'm sorry. I didn't mean to fall asleep. I don't know why I'm so tired. I guess maybe I'm still trying to catch up from last week."

"Don't apologize. I'm sure you being pregnant adds to it. I can't wait to raise our children together. The woods surrounding the cabin will be a perfect place for you to teach this little one how to use and master his powers, don't you think?" I asked as I gently placed a hand on Arin's stomach.

"How did you know?"

"Sorry, Arin. I sort of let that spill earlier," Elliot told his brother with an apologetic look.

"It's quite alright. I'm anxious to meet him. And I've told you before, no matter what, I'm going to love each and every one of our children."

"Thank you. I didn't know if you'd be okay with having a warlock. We only got one somehow, and then knowing he's a warlock and not a bear, I didn't want to disappoint you."

"Sweetheart, you and our children could never disappoint me," I said as I wrapped my arms around my mate and drew him close. I gave him a gentle kiss and then looked towards the other three.

"Arin, it's good to see that you're well on your way to mastering another power," Edison said as he smiled at his son. He walked up to us and wrapped both of us in his arms and gave us a quick hug, and then kissed first Arin's forehead, and then mine. I didn't quite know what to make of it.

"What do you mean, Papa?"

"Have you not successfully teleported both you and your mate to several different places over the past few days?"

"Yes. But we don't always land successfully. And when we do, I'm sure it's just a fluke."

"Only if you lose that faith and confidence that you've seemed to gain. Your One is very important to you and your powers now. Just remember that."

"I will, Papa."

Edison looked at us again before he turned and smiled at Troy and Elliot, and then he was gone.

"Yeah, that really is going to take some getting used to. It's just different when you're the one being poofed somewhere. But when Edison just pops in and out, it can be a little unnerving," I said to the others. Troy agreed by nodding his head, Arin and Elliot just laughed.

"Okay, we should probably get some work accomplished. Are you staying with me, or are you going back with your brother?"

"I need to get back. Papa was going to help me with some things."

"Alright. Don't forget, you're always welcome here. I'll be home early because I can't see us staying late. It's not exactly tourist season right now. There's still snow on the ground and that doesn't make for happy campers or hikers." I looked at Arin and gave him a quick kiss before him and his brother both vanished.

"Yeah, definitely going to take time to get used to. Although, when they do it, it's not quite as unsettling." It was certainly going to be interesting being in a family of warlocks now.

Troy outright laughed and I quickly joined him. Life in Montana was looking up. I had a mate and a little warlock on the way. What more could I ask for?

Arin — 10

Ryker and I were settling into domestic life quite well. I was halfway through my pregnancy now and had what Ryker loved to call a cute little bump. Elliot and Arik just glared and grumbled at me and said it wasn't fair. Somehow it was my fault that I was having a single instead of multiples. Oh well. Sitting on the back deck, enjoying the warm May sun, I looked out at the forest and got to thinking about Ryker and his parents.

"You're quiet. Is everything okay?" Ryker asked.

I gazed up at the man, the bear that was now mine for the rest of our lives. And he needed to know it was going to be a long life now. "Your parents, I saw them in your memories, are you not close?"

"Not really, no. They left when I was just barely old enough to be on my own. Before then, they were what I'd call inattentive I guess. They showed up in Alaska from time to time, but never stayed long. Over the years, we've grown apart and they're basically strangers now. They never really seemed to want me or anything to do with me. I honestly think they had me simply because they didn't realize they were going to meet their mate so they weren't prepared with suppressants and along I came five months later." Ryker sat beside me, wrapped an arm around me, and gave me a tight squeeze.

"I don't really understand. War and Troy are both insanely crazy about their cubs. And War said it was difficult for female bears to have cubs."

"It can be—which is most likely part of the reason why I'm an only child. My parents love to travel and once I was old enough, they started travelling. I don't even know where they are right now."

"Wow. That's just crazy. You're happy about the baby, right?"

"Are you kidding? I'm ecstatic. I can't wait to meet him. And if you're willing, I want to have more. As many as you want. If you only want the one, I'm good."

"Ryker?"

"Yeah?"

"Relax. I want more. I grew up with a twin and Elliot still around. I don't want our children to not have that. If the fates bless us with more, I'm willing."

"I love you, Arin."

"I know."

"Good. And no matter what, our little guy will grow up with five older cousins here in the den."

"Oh hey! I didn't think about that. Wow. Yeah, he's going to have plenty of playmates."

"Yes, he is. Why don't we go upstairs and take a nap? I'm getting that you're feeling a little tired, and you're really relaxed here."

"I'm sorry. I don't want to be so sleepy. But I need to talk to you about something first. You realize that when you claimed me your lifespan was extended to match mine, right?"

"Yeah, sweetheart, I did. I figured out that Edison was super old and assumed that all of his children would be as well. As for you being so tired, don't worry about it. Edison said it's normal, and there's nothing to be worried about."

"Are you sure you don't mind?"

"About the extended lifetime? No. Why would I mind? I get to spend that much more time with you. If you're referring to taking a nap, I'm always up for curling up with you. Unless you don't want me with you; but I happen to like holding you."

"Then, yes, a nap sounds wonderful. But don't feel like you have to stay in bed with me the whole time. If you wake up before me, do what you have to."

"Alright, I will."

By the time we were settled in bed, I could barely keep my eyes open and was asleep in no time. When I woke again, I realized it was late afternoon by the light coming in through the windows.

"I'm in the office, sweetheart. I've gone through all of my emails and let your dads know that we'd come to dinner next weekend."

"I'm sorry I slept so long. What time is it?"

"Just after four. Do you want me to come back upstairs?"

"No. I'll be right down, just give me a few minutes to go to the bathroom."

Ryker chuckled and I heard it through our bond so he had to have sent it to me. I sent a picture back of me rolling my eyes, and he laughed so loud I heard him through the open bedroom door. I quickly made my way to the bathroom and took care of business and then went in search of my One.

"Hey, beautiful. What would you like for dinner?"

"I know it's your bear pushing you, but I swear, it seems like all we do is sleep and eat. If I get a snack, can we maybe go for a drive or a walk in the woods?"

"Drive, yes. Walk, no. Not unless we go over to War's. Sorry, I talked to Edison earlier and he said the other bears are still in the area but they're not moving much. I just don't want to take any chances with you or our little guy. The protection spell is only on the cabin and the immediate grounds, but the woods weren't possible. And until we know more about exactly who's out there and what their plans are, I'm not comfortable with taking you out there."

"But I'd never let anything happen to either of us. I can protect us while out there."

"I know you can, sweetheart. But if they catch you off-guard, then it's possible that you and our little guy could get hurt. My bear and I can't handle that. I'm sorry."

"It's okay. I know we've only been together for a couple months, but I hope that in time, you'll see that I'm not quite the bumbling mess my brothers think I am."

"Hey, come here," Ryker said, reaching for me. He pulled me over onto his lap, and I looked into his beautiful brown eyes. "You are amazing. I don't think you're a bumbling mess. And I'm sure your brothers don't think that either. I know they've picked on you in the past but that was just that. I've had more than one conversation with certain members of your family about that."

"They've always been supportive, but they've picked on me so many times about how much of a mess I am. It wasn't until just before Elliot found Troy that I could even levitate anything. Elliot was with me in Amherst and helped me so much."

"See. Do you really think they see you as a bumbling mess?"

"No, but they're so much better than me." I looked down at my lap and picked off a non-existent piece of lint from my pants.

"Arin, sweetheart, look at me."

When I did, I saw nothing but love and understanding in Ryker's eyes.

"Look and see so you'll understand exactly how I feel."

When I did, I gasped. Never before had I ever felt so much love, devotion, and understanding. Ryker completely believed in me and my abilities, and that was such a confidence boost that I couldn't contain my excitement. I reached around his neck and pulled him in for a kiss. After things went much further than I had intended, I broke away so I could look into his eyes again.

"Thank you. You don't know how much it means to me that you believe in me so much."

"Sweetheart, how could I not? Now, since your stomach is quietly grumbling, let's get you that snack and then we'll go for a drive. I'll show you around the lake before dinner."

"That sounds good."

"Great. Now snack. You need one. My bear is getting upset and is being a cranky ass."

I nodded in agreement and got up off Ryker's lap and walked to the kitchen with him right behind me. Once I had a snack secured in my hands, he nodded and led me out to his truck and then we were on our way. Troy had shown us around the lake a few times, and I'd explored it on my own more than once. It was different to be seeing it with my own fated One though.

"You seem happy about work, but I don't think I've ever asked if you enjoy your job?"

"Yes, very much so. My bear loves to be outside, and even though he doesn't always get to take his form as often as he'd like, he's happy and content when I'm outside. What about you? Have you enjoyed working on healing with Edison?"

"Yes. I know with your shifter healing you wouldn't necessarily need that particular power, but it's nice to have it. I'm really close, but not quite there yet. I get frustrated, and I have to stop and remind myself that I'm young, very young for a warlock. It's unusual for warlocks to find their One so early in life and I seem to forget that sometimes."

"I have every faith that you will. So, subject change. You've already been to the ranger station where Troy, Jai, and I work." Ryker pointed to the building in front of us. It looked like a log and stone cabin. It wasn't overly large, but it was plenty big enough for the three of them. It helped that they all got along well. "There's somewhere I want to show you. It's one of my favorite spots at the lake."

"I can't wait. What makes it one of your favorites?"

"Honestly? It reminds me of home. It looks a lot like the area near where I grew up. I don't know, I guess in some ways, I miss Alaska."

"Do you want to go back?"

"No. You're here and your family is here. I'd never ask you to leave them. I'm happy here."

"No, I meant, did you want to go back and visit? Elliot took Troy to the cabin he bought in Alaska to be claimed. Do you want to go to Alaska? I can have us there in about two seconds."

Ryker just looked at me, then glanced back out the windshield of the truck and then back at me.

"Are you serious? I guess I never thought about that. You can, can't you?"

"Yeah. We can go to Alaska right now if you want. I just need you to show me exactly where. I've seen so much of Alaska through our bond, but I need to know where specifically you want to go."

When Ryker sent me images of him in his bear form running on a rocky beach in the water, then the large cabin he lived in and the ranger station he used to work at, I knew exactly where he wanted to go. In an instant, I had the truck parked, turned off, and we were standing on the shore in Alaska where Ryker had grown up. Ryker's excitement, happiness, and gratitude poured into me through our bond, and I looked over at my One and just smiled.

"Go on. I can't wait to see your bear running in the water like you showed me in your visions. I love your bear. He makes me feel good and safe, and I enjoy spending time with him."

"Thank you. This is wonderful. I didn't realize how much I missed this place. If you ever want to go back to Amherst, I'll understand."

"Nope. I don't miss it. It's too crowded and nothing at all like Honey Creek. But thank you. Now strip, sexy, so I can meet that bear of yours again." Where was all of this confidence coming from? I'd never been this bold or assertive before in my life. But as I watched my fated One remove all of his clothing and then I was once again standing next to my giant Kodiak bear, life just felt right. I sighed as I buried my face in Ryker's furry neck. "Go on. Run. Be free and enjoy yourself. It makes me so happy to see you like that. I love you, Ryker."

"I love you too, Arin. So much." Then Ryker was off, racing down the pebbled beach in the very edge of the surf. I couldn't help but smile, laugh, and enjoy how happy he was. I'd somehow done that for him.

I looked around and could see why Ryker loved it here so much. We'd been mated for almost three months now. Why hadn't I brought him back before? I knew I needed to do this on a regular basis. He was so happy and carefree here. Troy and Elliot spent time in Alaska on a regular basis, what was to say that we couldn't?

Ryker — 11

It had been months since I'd ran on this beach, but it wasn't something I'd ever forget. And I knew I needed to make sure I thanked my amazing mate for giving me such a wonderful gift. Never did I think I'd be able to return here in the blink of an eye. After running down the beach, my bear was happy and content to turn around and return to our pregnant mate. We found him sitting on a large bolder, looking out at the Shelikof Straight.

I immediately shifted when I got close enough. I didn't stop to pull on the clothes he was holding out to me though. I simply tugged him into my arms and kissed him with all of the love I could. When he moaned, I finally backed away, although just slightly.

"Thank you. This was a wonderful gift, and I'll never forget it. But surely you must be cold sitting on the boulder."

"No. I heated it. And I'm not the one who's naked, outside, in Alaska in May."

When I looked down, I was no longer naked thanks to the help of my mate. "You really are amazing, you know that, right?"

"You're biased, but I'll take it."

"You're absolutely right. I'm biased because I do have an amazing mate." I gave Arin another quick kiss and then took a step back from him. "So I guess it's time to head back to Montana then."

"If you want. We can head home or you could show me around for a bit. It's up to you."

"My old place is just on the other side of the cove down there. I never sold it and a friend was going to keep an eye on it for me. Somehow I knew I wouldn't be moving back here, but I still couldn't bring myself to get rid of it."

"Well, if it's open, would you mind showing me?"

"Of course. You okay to walk? I can give you a piggy back ride if you'd like."

"Why is it that you feel that I can't walk all of a sudden? I'm pregnant but that doesn't mean I'm unable to walk." Arin glared at me, but before I could respond, we were standing outside my childhood home.

"Okay, I should be used to that by now but I'm not. Maybe a little head's up next time?"

"Wow. I've seen this place in your memories, but it didn't seem this big."

"I don't really know why my parents had such a large home. It was only ever just the three of us and I really don't think they wanted me, let alone more cubs. This house is perfect for a family with several children. Maybe I hung onto it because I knew I'd be meeting you soon."

"I'm sorry. I didn't mean to bring up bad memories."

"You didn't. I have a lot of good memories here in this house too. You want to see the inside?"

"Can I?"

"Of course." I pulled out my keys as we walked up the porch, but as we approached the front door swung open and there stood my friend, Aspen.

"Well, my fates. The last thing I expected was to find you here! I thought you moved down to Montana?"

"Aspen, what are you doing here? And I did. I'd like you to meet my mate, Arin. Sweetheart, this is my friend, Aspen, who I was just telling you about," I told Arin as I ushered him up the stairs.

"Yeah, about that. I was going to call you, but I never got around to it. But congratulations on finding your mate. And it looks like he's pregnant too?"

"Yes. About halfway. We're excited. But you want to tell me what's going on?"

"Yeah, can we go inside?" Aspen asked while pointing over his shoulder but looking over mine. What was going on?

"Ryker, is he okay? He seems nervous."

"I know, sweetheart. He had said he'd keep an eye on the cabin for me but that's it. Last I knew, he was living at home with his parents. But by the look of things, it's obvious he's been staying here."

"Alright, Aspen. Spill it."

"Yeah, so you know how my parents have been pushing for me to find my mate, right?"

"Riiiight." I did *not* like where this was going already.

"Well, they started pushing me to leave to go find him. Then all of a sudden, one night at dinner, they told me I had to leave. I had to set out and get away from here and look for my mate. I honestly don't know what's going on. I just don't get it, Ryker. I mean, aren't you supposed to find your mate near your den?"

"Aspen, there has to be some other reason why they asked you to leave. I mean, there's something else going on."

"I don't know, Ryker. They've changed. A lot. I've seen a strange alpha around a few times, but he doesn't stay long, and I've never actually talked to him."

"When did all of this happen?" Arin asked.

"Last week. I've only been here about a week. And if I wasn't so concerned, I'd try to go further, but I don't have a lot of money saved. What I had was in the bank in town, but since I'm not sure what's going on, I don't know where I should go. My parents aren't acting like themselves at all. As for mates, I'm just like you,

Ryker. I'd rather be without my entire life than to settle for someone that isn't my fated mate. There's no point otherwise."

"Sweetheart, what do you say we take Aspen back to Montana with us? They won't think to look for him there; his trail will be cold."

"I was just about to ask if we should. War and Arik have tons of space at their place."

"Yes, they do, but so do we."

"Yeah, but wouldn't he be more comfortable in one of the cabins at War's?"

"Well, maybe, but he's my friend, and I'd like to look after him for a few days. I'd really like to help him figure this out."

"Yeah, sure."

I gave Arin a long look. Was he upset for some reason?

"I love you. You know that, right?"

"Yep."

"You two are quiet. Everything okay?"

"Hey, Aspen. What do you think about coming back to Montana with us? War, he's the Alpha and is mated to Arin's brother. He's nice and he's fair; I'm sure he'd accept you into the den with no issues."

"I don't want to cause problems in your den."

"You wouldn't. Besides we already have problems, but we also have something nobody expects," I told him.

"What's that?"

"Arin and his family."

"I'm not following. How are—"

Before Aspen could finish the question, we were landing in a heap in War's back room. I just barely had enough time to cradle Arin's reentry, but I noticed he was hovering just above me and wasn't touching me. I looked around and saw Edison standing off to the side with a raised eyebrow. That explained why Arin didn't fall. Me and Aspen though, that was a different story. We were in a heap on the floor.

"Okay, what was that and where are we? What's just happened? Have I lost my mind and gone crazy?"

I turned my head and laughed. I held out my arms for Arin who gently floated down to me. When he landed on me, I wrapped my arms around him and kissed his forehead before I turned to Aspen. "Welcome to the family, Aspen. I guess you didn't realize that my mate is a warlock. That's his papa over there," I said as I nodded towards Edison who was now sitting on the couch with Wallace. Aspen's face went white as a sheet, and he scrambled to his backside and tried to crab-walk backwards.

"What the hell, Ryker? Dude over there is scary as fuck!"

I busted out laughing; I couldn't help it. Poor Edison. I knew he got that a lot, and he was intimidating all the time. The power just radiated off of him. But he got up and strode right over to

Aspen who was crab-walking even faster trying to get away. Edison just held out his hand to help my friend up.

"You have nothing to worry about here. We're friendly enough," Edison told him. I laughed louder and Wallace joined me. Meanwhile, Arin, my adorable mate, glared at me.

"Behave. I already messed things up with my reentry."

"No, mate. You didn't. Like always, you've done everything just right for you. I'll take you being in my arms any opportunity I can get. But we should probably get up off of the floor."

I gave Arin a quick kiss and then we both sat up, and I watched as Aspen got up without Edison's assistance.

"Really, Aspen, Papa won't hurt you. You're not one of the bad guys. And even then, there's still rules as to what he can and can't do."

"You! You did this. Where are we? Ryker? What kind of twilight zone are we in?"

"Seriously, Aspen, just calm down."

"Calm down? You're mated to a warlock, and you want me to calm down?"

"Yes. Calm down. There is *nothing* wrong with my being mated to a warlock." Just then, War and Arik came in with their twins to see what the commotion was.

Aspen at least looked embarrassed about his comment. "You're right. I'm sorry, Arin. I really have nothing against you.

I've never met a warlock before and this guy is scary, seriously frightening." Aspen started to creep around Edison who was still standing there laughing.

"Everyone, this is Aspen. He grew up near me in Kodiak. He was having some issues with his parents so we offered him a safe place to land. Aspen, this is everyone."

My poor friend was completely overwhelmed. He looked from War to Wallace to Edison then at me. "This is crazy. No wonder nobody messes with you. Scary dude has a scary tiger that I'd swear is his mate."

"He's my One, actually, but yes. Scary dude has a big, bad tiger for a One," Edison said and then laughed so hard he bent over at the waist. "Ryker, I really like him. We've got to keep him around."

Aspen's eyes got huge, and I decided to give him just a little relief. "He'll stay with me and Arin, but I'm sure you'll see him on a regular basis."

"Hi, Aspen. I'm Arik. I'm Arin's twin and Alpha Mate for our den. Welcome."

"Hi, Arik. Nice to meet you. You're a tiger too?"

"Yes. I'm the only one of their children that ended up a shifter. All of my brothers are warlocks like our papa."

"Okay. I think I need to sit down," Aspen said just before he plopped down in the middle of the floor and looked up at us."

"You'll fit in just fine here, Aspen. I promise. War's a great Alpha. You'll see," I said as I crouched down near my friend. "You okay? I can have Arin take us back to Alaska if you want."

"No. I'm good. I just…" Aspen trailed off as his eyes got huge again. I looked over my shoulder and laughed outright. Poor Aspen. He was completely overwhelmed by everyone.

"That's Troy. He works with me at the ranger station. The tall, dark-haired guy with him is his mate, Elliot. Elliot is—"

"One of them," Aspen said as he pointed to Edison and Arin.

I got up off of the floor and went to Arin's waiting arms. I wrapped him up and gave him another kiss before turning to look back at my friend.

"This is going to take some getting used to," Aspen said as he looked around the room. We grew up in a very small den of only five families, and Aspen's family joined the den when I was already old enough to be out on my own. He was so adorable as a little Kodiak cub running around the beach. Granted, there weren't five couples with us now, but with Edison, Wallace, and War, they were so much *more* intense.

"Don't worry. You can hide out at our cabin with me I suppose. Ryker goes to work in the morning, and I usually come here to work on my powers with Papa and Elliot, but I can hang out with you at our cabin if you want."

"Can we, you know, poof back and get my things?"

At Aspen's use of War's chosen word for teleporting, the entire room lost it, War included.

"That won't be necessary. I already sent them to the spare room at our place. Your stuff is waiting for you there," Arin told him with a smile.

"Really? Thanks. Can we maybe, go there?" Aspen asked. "I just need some time to process…things."

"Sure can," I told him before looking down at Arin.

"He's overwhelmed. Can you get us out of here?"

"Yeah. I'll send the two of you to the truck, and you can chat with him on the way home. I'll be there when you get there."

"Perfect. Love you."

"Love you, too, Ryker."

I kissed Arin's nose before Aspen and I were sent off to the truck. I really did love my mate.

Arin — 12

Poor Aspen. He was so overwhelmed. He'd been raised on an island in Alaska and had come from an incredibly small den. War's den used to be equally small. It had grown over the last couple years with all of the new arrivals and mates showing up. I kept reminding myself that the fates knew what they were doing.

"Where did they go?" War asked.

"I sent them to the truck. I'm not sure what exactly is going on yet, but I know Aspen is essentially homeless because his parents told him he needed to leave to find his mate. He mentioned some strange alpha hanging around as well."

"That doesn't make sense. Who does that to their child?" Dad asked. I knew he was angry when Papa went over and ran his hand up and down Dad's arm.

"We all know that. And Ryker said there had to be something else going on, but Aspen said he honestly didn't know. He packed up everything he could carry and was hiding out in Ryker's cabin he still has in Alaska. Ryker offered to bring him back here with us, so here we are."

"You don't seem overly happy about that. Do you want me to look into it?" Papa asked.

"Would you? Did you get enough of his aura to trace back where to go?"

"Really?" Papa asked with a raised eyebrow.

"What? I swear, I've lost my mind during this pregnancy. I can't remember things anymore," I basically all but grumbled to myself. When I looked up, Papa was smiling affectionately at me, and Elliot was trying to not laugh. "Shut up," I said to my older brother.

"It'll get better. I promise. But tell me, you're in your second trimester of your pregnancy. Are you sure you two want a third living with you?" Papa asked.

"I mentioned having him stay here in one of the cabins, but Ryker said how we had enough room. He's right. We do. But I don't think he was really thinking about how that would affect our bedroom activities. Let's just say they're all but going to stop. There is no way I'm having sex with him with his friend in the cabin."

"You say that now. Just wait until you get home and curl up with your One. Trust me on that," Elliot told me. I knew he was probably right, but I couldn't do it. It was just...no.

"I'd better get home. Papa, I'll see you at some point tomorrow, right?"

"Yes. I'm going to head up to Alaska for a few and see what I can find out, and I can come by tomorrow and let you know if I discovered anything."

"Thanks, Papa." I gave my dads hugs and then teleported home. I knew Ryker was most likely hungry and his bear was going to push for me to eat so I prepared a beef stew and homemade bread for dinner. It was on the table and ready to eat when Ryker and Aspen walked through the door. I was just reorganizing things when Ryker walked up behind me and wrapped his arms around my waist and gave me a quick kiss.

"Thanks for dinner, sweetheart. It smells wonderful."

"It's not much, but it'll be filling. And I knew your bear was going to be pushing for me to eat. He always is."

"I can't help it. You know that."

"Yeah, I do. Wash your hands and we'll eat."

Ryker went to the kitchen sink and washed his hands. Aspen was right beside him and when they were finished, they both sat at the table. I took the third seat, the one furthest from Ryker, since Aspen sat in mine. Throughout dinner, I sat listening to Ryker and Aspen get caught up, and when dinner was finally over, I quickly cleaned up the dinner mess and excused myself to our room. I was more than ready for some silence. Aspen could certainly talk.

Several hours later, Ryker came into our room and crawled into bed beside me. When he started nibbling on my neck, I rolled over and pushed him away.

"Hey. What's wrong? I can feel your need through my mate mark, sweetheart. Why are you pushing me away?"

"You can't be serious."

"Yes. I can seriously feel it. And I know the second trimester of your pregnancy is one that we've both enjoyed, immensely."

"You're right. We have. But that was before you wanted your friend to come back with us. There is no way I'm doing anything with you while he's staying here. There is nothing quiet about us, and I don't know him, and therefore, if you need relief, you know where the shower is." I rolled over and did my best to try to fall asleep. I knew I was being unfair and unreasonable, but I was horny and pregnant, and my One had just invited his friend to live with us. It wasn't really an issue, and I'd get over it, but I needed just a little more time.

I eventually dozed off, and when I woke up the next morning, Ryker was still asleep beside me. After quickly taking a shower and getting ready for the day, I made my way downstairs and to the kitchen. I allowed myself one cup of coffee now that I was pregnant, and I savored it before I was interrupted by Ryker and Aspen coming down the stairs together. I swear, if I didn't know that Ryker was completely devoted to me, I'd be jealous. As it was, I was just uncomfortable.

"Good morning, sweetheart. Why didn't you wake me up? Have you already eaten?"

"I didn't wake you up because you were up half the night tossing and turning. No, I haven't eaten, I thought I'd have breakfast with my brothers this morning."

"Arin, you okay?"

"Yep. You two enjoy your day at the office. I'll see you for dinner." I gave a stunned-looking Ryker a quick kiss and then I was gone. Yes, it was incredibly childish of me, but I needed to talk to my Papa as soon as possible. When I arrived on his and Dad's doorstep, he flung the door open before I could even knock.

"What's wrong? I can tell something's upsetting you," Papa asked as he ushered me inside.

"Sweetheart, what's going on?"

I held up a finger to Papa to talk to Ryker before I answered Papa.

"Sorry, Ryker. I'm a little preoccupied right now. We can talk later if you're not busy."

"I'm never too busy for you. But I can tell something is upsetting you."

"I'm just busy and have a lot to do. Enjoy your day and I'll see you later. Now, sorry, but I really need to concentrate."

"Arin, tell me what's wrong. First, I had to try ignoring the vibrations of my mating mark all night and then you rushed out this morning."

"Not now, Ryker." I all but yelled at my One. I was being completely unfair and pissy, and I knew it but I just couldn't right now.

"Honestly, I thought Ryker would agree to have Aspen stay here in one of the cabins but he didn't. He seems to want him at our place. But it's uncomfortable for me. I don't like the idea of him knowing what we're doing, or the fact that he can hear us. He came to bed well after midnight last night. I don't have any problems with him catching up with his friend, but I'm just uncomfortable. And before you say anything, I know I'm being unreasonable, but I can't seem to help it. And these vibrations that are going through my body and steadily getting stronger are really starting to get annoying."

"Sweetheart. I'm on my way to War's. I'll be there in about ten minutes. We need to talk."

I rolled my eyes and held up my finger again to let Papa know I had to answer Ryker.

"Go to work, Ryker. I'm going with Papa and Dad to Alaska to see what can be found out about Aspen's parents."

"What? No. We need to talk."

"Then it'll have to wait. You have work to do and so do I. With Papa, in Alaska, it'll be a good time for me to practice some of my magic anyway."

"What's going on?"

"Really? You shouldn't have to ask. Now go to work. I'll talk to you later. Stop distracting me."

I heard Ryker growl through our bond, but I ignored him and looked over at Papa and Dad. They both had a look of amusement on their faces.

"You know, he might not ever figure it out if you don't tell him what's wrong," Dad said while smiling at me.

"Yeah, I know. If he doesn't figure it out by dinner, I'll let him know. I'm not upset with him, just really uncomfortable. I know I shouldn't be. I know that mates acting as mates tend to do is a natural thing. It's me, not him. And I know he means nothing by it, but he didn't even say anything last night when Aspen took my seat at the table. I sat at the other end."

"Arin! Why are you blocking me? We're in the truck. We'll be there in a few minutes."

"Sorry, Ryker. We're going to Alaska. Go to work."

"Papa, we need to go to Alaska, now. I'm not ready to have this out with Ryker just yet."

Before I could blink again, Dad, Papa, and I were all on the very same beach Ryker and I were on just yesterday afternoon. Only this time, it was still dark out.

"Ryker's cabin is just over there," I said as I pointed to his childhood home. In a blink, we were on his front porch and then Papa had the door open. Once inside, everything looked just as it did the day before.

"I've picked up a stronger sense of Aspen's aura here that I can follow. You want to go with us or do you want to stay here and explore?"

"I'm really torn. I know Ryker's pissed. I've blocked him somewhat and he's upset. He can still sense me, but I'm not responding and I've all but muted him because he started yelling."

"Hang on," Papa said just before Elliot appeared.

"Oh, gorgeous cabin. Where are we?"

"Ryker's cabin in Alaska. Could you please have your One have a *talk* with Ryker? He seems to be clueless at the moment."

"Sure thing. Although, I want to come back to this place."

"You and me both. We weren't here but just a few minutes yesterday," I told Elliot as I looked around. The cabin really was beautiful. And it certainly was set up for a family with lots of children.

"Okay, I'm off. Good luck you three. I'll make sure Troy has a long discussion with Ryker."

"Yeah, could you maybe somehow make sure Aspen doesn't hear it? I don't know, send them out into the middle of the forest or something?"

"I will. Hang in there, Arin. I know Ryker didn't realize how he was hurting you."

"I know he didn't as well. I'm just trying to figure out how to handle all this now."

"Don't worry. You two will figure it out. Now, I left my One at home with our triplets all by himself. Although he's perfectly capable of handling them all on his own, it's time for their bottles so I'd better get back and help."

With that Elliot was gone, and I was left standing in Ryker's cabin with our dads.

"So, what's the plan?" I asked.

"Go to Aspen's house and see if we can sort out this mystery. They won't be able to detect us so it'll be as if we're not even there."

I nodded at Papa and before I even had a moment to think about it, we were standing in the middle of Aspen's home. Now I really wished I'd stayed in Montana and had a discussion with Ryker instead.

Ryker — 13

What the hell was going on? Why was Arin ignoring me? Our mate bond wasn't closed off, but it was almost like he wasn't hearing me. How could I fix it if I didn't know what was wrong with him? And if the intensity of the vibrations through my mate mark were anything near what he was feeling throughout his entire body, he needed me. He needed me last night, but for whatever reason, he said no. My bear and I simply didn't understand what was happening.

"Hey, Ryker. You got a minute?" Troy asked. I looked up at him but couldn't get a read on him.

"Yeah, sure. Come in and have a seat," I said as I gestured to the open chair beside Aspen across from my desk. He'd talked almost non-stop since Arin left this morning.

"Actually, would it be okay if you come with me? There's something out at the south beach I need to show you."

"Oh. Absolutely. Come on, Aspen. I guess you'll get to see the lake a little sooner than I had said."

"Sure thing." As Aspen got up from his chair, I could have sworn that Troy quietly growled before he turned and quickly left. By the time Aspen and I walked out of my office, Troy was standing in front of his desk next to both Elliot and Arik.

"There you are. Perfect timing. As Alpha Mate, I've come to welcome you to the den. If you'll come with us, we'll show you around and see about getting you settled in a little better," Arik said with a big smile on his face.

"Actually, I'm going to the lake with Ryker."

"Oh, we'll get there too. Elliot, shall we?" Arik asked just before looking at his brother, and after Elliot gave Troy a quick kiss, the three of them were gone.

I looked left and right and then at Troy, and yep, they were really gone.

"Okay, well that was odd, but that seems to be the norm this morning. You ready to go to the south beach?"

"Actually, no. Let's go into your office and have a chat. The south beach is fine as far as I know. Jai was going out to do rounds this morning. I was just trying to get you away from your shadow. We need to talk." Troy walked past me and back into my office without waiting.

"What do you mean my shadow? What's going on? Everyone is acting so strange this morning."

"How's Arin?" Troy asked as he sat down in the chair Aspen had just been in.

"You just saw him last night. He's good."

"Yeah? You sure?"

My bear and I got overly concerned at Troy's line of questioning. "Do you know something I don't? He took off this morning with his dads to go to Alaska. He hasn't closed our bond, but he's ignoring me. Isn't he okay?" My bear was about to burst out and race back to Alaska as fast as he could. I was almost positive Arin was okay, I'd know otherwise.

"Calm down. He's fine. Let me rephrase. How do you *think* Arin's doing?"

"I don't know. But you'd better start talking before you piss off my bear even more."

"Think about it, Ryker. What's changed in the last twenty-four hours?"

"Nothing. Except that Arin pulled away. Which is odd because I know he needs me, but he's denying us both."

Troy looked at the ceiling and seemed to be counting. Why was he doing that?

"What else?"

"Huh?" I was completely clueless.

"Yep, you're not getting it. Think, Ryker. What's changed all of a sudden?"

"The only other thing different is Asp...Shit!"

Troy was nodding his head with a big smile on his face.

"Aspen? Arin is upset about Aspen? Why?"

"Ryker, think about it. You know your mate better than anyone. But even I know that Arin, for all of his bubbly personality, when it comes down to it, he's shy. And you two are fairly newly mated. And you just brought an old friend home. An omega at that."

"Yeah, but Arin knows that he was my first. He knows there's never been anyone before him."

"Really? Wow. How...never mind, that's not important. The point is, he's shy. Think about that. He's still unsure about a lot of things. Even you were ripping us all a new one just a couple months ago about mentioning his struggles with his powers."

"Yeah, but that has nothing to do with him being shy. That's all a self-confidence issue. His brothers and some of the other warlocks in the coven made him self-conscious about not learning faster. That destroyed his focus."

"True. But what I was getting at was that you were his biggest champion just two and a half months ago. Now you've brought a stranger into your home. Tell me, did Arin say it was okay?"

"Well, yeah. He...shit. No, he suggested a cabin at War's. Wait. Is that why he turned me down last night? I know for a fact that he's in pain today because of it."

"Well, he's shy, Ryker. Do you think he wants a strange shifter hearing you knot him?"

"But that's not a big deal for us. We all have that hearing, and it's just natural."

"Fates help me," Troy said as he looked at the ceiling again. "Ryker, your mate isn't a shifter. He's a warlock. And a very young one at that. From what Elliot said, it's almost unheard of for a warlock to find their One so young."

"Yeah, Arin said the same thing. What of it?"

"Okay, I'll spell it out since your brain seems to be missing this morning."

I growled at Troy who looked at me and laughed. But then he held up a finger and started counting.

"One, you have a very young, new mate. Two, he's a warlock so things are already going to be a little different for him than you. Three, you brought home a stranger to him, and it's made him uncomfortable. Four, said stranger took his seat last night at dinner and then you two proceeded to chat as if he wasn't there. Five, he went to bed without you, and it was well after midnight before you came to bed. Need I go further?"

I banged my head on the desk. No wonder. Shit. I didn't even think about how Arin would feel about having someone from my old den at the cabin with us, especially an omega.

"Ryker? Is he talking to you yet? If not, Elliot said to let him know and he'd let Edison know."

"Do I want to know about that? Arin said they can't communicate like we do."

Troy laughed at me. "I actually think he was referring to just texting."

"Let me check," I told Troy before trying to see if I could get Arin to respond. So far this morning, nothing. *"Sweetheart? You listening? I'm sorry. I can't tell you how sorry I am. I'm an idiot. Please, sweetheart, answer me."*

I sat there waiting, and still nothing. I looked at Troy and was about to let him know that Arin was still not responding when all of a sudden, he did.

"Ryker? Please. I need you. Can you meet me at home?"

"Yes. I'll be there within ten minutes. I'm leaving now."

"Something's wrong. I gotta go. I'll be back later after I find out what's going on." My eyes met Troy's and he nodded in understanding.

"Don't worry about it. Things are still really slow here. I'll fill out any reports that need to be finished. Just take care of Arin; he's your number one priority."

"Thanks, Troy," I said as I got up and rushed out of the office.

I grabbed my pack on the way out the door and then I was on my way to my mate. The last thing I expected to find when I got home was a distraught Arin in our cabin. I rushed to him on the couch and gathered him into my arms.

"Sweetheart, what's wrong?" I asked as I brushed my fingers through his red hair. His bright blue eyes were red and puffy from where he'd been crying, and it broke my heart and upset my bear that our mate was so upset.

"So much: I'm emotional, I'm horny, I'm being unfair, and they're all gone."

"Okay, I understand the first two. How are you unfair? And who's gone?"

"I'm being immature with Aspen. When it comes down to it, I'm jealous. He's never done anything to me, but yet I'm still acting like an ass. And I hurt you because of it. I ignored you when you wanted to talk to me. And Aspen's parents and the other alpha are just gone. Papa said it was like they simply disappeared. He was going to follow their auras and see where it led him, but they're missing."

"Are they? Can he tell if they're…"?

"As of right now, he said they're still alive. He's just trying to find them. He sent me home. I should have spoken up last night when you asked me what was wrong. I'm ashamed of how I've behaved. I haven't been a very good mate to you, and I'm truly sorry for that."

"What are you talking about? You're a wonderful mate. I love you so much, sweetheart. Now, should we go talk to Aspen? We need to let him know about his parents."

"Papa said this afternoon would be best. Elliot and Arik are going to show him around and try to get him to agree to one of the cabins near War and Arik's."

"I'm really sorry about all that. I didn't even think how it might affect you when I offered to bring him back here."

"Why would you? It shouldn't be an issue at all. I need to get over myself and not let it bother me."

"Okay, how about this? We're both still learning about this whole being mated thing, and we both need to learn to work on some things. We're going to learn together; how does that sound?"

"I think that sounds wonderful. I love you, Ryker. Thank you for putting up with me and for not giving up."

"Sweetheart, I'll never give up on us. You're mine. Now, how about a nap? You tossed and turned most of the night, and I think I only finally dozed off as the sun was starting to come up."

"I'm sorry. That's all my fault. I shouldn't have denied you last night," Arin said as he ran his fingers up and down my chest.

"Hmm, well, I should have asked what was wrong. I knew through our bond you needed me, but we do have the cabin to ourselves now. There's nobody here to hear us and you can be as loud as you like."

Suddenly, I found myself in our bedroom, naked and on our bed with my equally naked mate on top of me. When his mouth latched onto mine, I moaned and then got a whiff of his slick as it started to drip out of his hole.

"Want you, sweetheart. Please say yes."

"Yes, Ryker. Need you so much. Make me feel good. Make the ache stop."

I quickly flipped us and once Arin was on his back, I zeroed in on his mating bite and sucked, hard. I'd only ever been sweet and gentle with Arin, but I knew he needed more this time and that's exactly what I gave him. When he shouted my name, I smelled his release before I felt the warm wetness between our bodies.

I kissed my way down his body, licking up his release before I gave his softening cock a quick lick which caused him to moan and beg for more.

"Ryker. Please. I feel so empty."

The pulsing in my mating mark had steadily increased since we'd gotten to the bedroom, and I knew it had to be twice as intense for Arin since he felt the vibrations everywhere. I grabbed his slender body and after gently lifting his hips, I thrust into him in one quick push. Almost immediately, I started to feel my knot inflate and I pumped faster. Arin had us levitating off of the bed, and when I pushed one last time and stuck, he shouted and screamed my name once again. Between us, his dick started pulsing and painting his chest while mine throbbed and filled his warm channel with my release.

It had taken some getting used to, but I was more than comfortable with levitating in the air while Arin was stuck on my knot. I rolled, putting him above me, and then he slowly lowered us to the bed.

"Love you, sweetheart," I said as I kissed Arin's sweaty forehead. He was quietly snoring above me. The vibrations in my mate mark once again, gentle and soft.

Arin — 14

I was so warm and comfortable. I could smell Ryker's scent in my nose, and when I moved slightly, he groaned and tightened his arms around me. So I was in Ryker's arms, and we were naked. Judging by the light coming in through the windows, it was the middle of the day.

"You're thinking way too loud, sweetheart. Yes, it's probably the middle of the day, but who cares."

I couldn't help it, I giggled at that. Now that I was more awake, I remembered the crazy morning I'd had as well as the sweaty makeup sex that followed. It shouldn't have been needed though.

"Stop. I've already said you're thinking too loud. It's not your fault and anytime we make love, it's a good thing."

Ryker pushed back from me and looked down into my eyes. "You know how much I love you."

"I do and I love you, too. Thank you for cleaning us up. I guess I fell asleep."

"No problem. I like taking care of you. Now, let's get through the shower and then head over to War's for lunch. Hopefully, Edison is back and has some news for us."

"Mmm, a shower sounds nice."

"It does, doesn't it?" Ryker said just before he rolled out of bed and then reached over and swept me up into his arms. I may have squeaked a little, but I'd never actually confirm that.

"You know I can walk, right? You have a thing about carrying me. You offered to carry me yesterday as well."

"What can I say? I just really like having you in my arms." Ryker gave me a lingering, sweet kiss before he gently set me down on the bathroom floor. He reached in and turned on the water, and we both climbed in and under the warm spray. After we both quickly washed, we got out, dried off, and got dressed.

"You realize we've most likely missed lunch, right?"

"Yes, I do. But I also know that you can always just fix us lunch. Or if you'd like, I'm more than willing to cook for you here before we go," Ryker said. He'd cooked for me many times since we'd claimed each other. It seemed to make his bear incredibly happy, and he was a great cook. But when you've lived over a century, it was almost a given.

"I haven't heard anything from Papa yet, so maybe we could have lunch here? We didn't really get to talk too much earlier. We got distracted."

"We did. But I knew you were upset, and in distracting you, I accomplished two things."

"Yeah? What?"

"I got your mind off of what you thought was an issue, and I was able to take care of your needs. Arin, please don't ever walk around upset with me like that. If you have a question, or you're displeased with something, let me know. I can read your mind, but only what you want me to see. I need to know when something's bothering you. I can't fix it otherwise."

"I'm really sorry. I'll try to remember that. I'm still getting used to having someone else that always wants to please me."

"Sweetheart, I'll always want you happy. And no matter what, I'll always love you and support you. Alright?"

I nodded at Ryker in understanding. We were interrupted by his phone chiming with an incoming text message.

"It's Troy. He said your dads are back and asked if we'd come to War's. They want to talk to all of us at once."

"Well, I guess lunch will have to wait."

"Only until we get to War's. You will eat, pregnant mate of mine."

"You and your constant need to feed me. Although, I will say this, I've had it so much easier than Elliot did. He was so sick with the triplets. Troy went crazy because he couldn't keep anything down. Papa kept reassuring him, but it didn't work. At times, I don't know how Elliot put up with Troy."

"Just wait. I'll get there too. We simply can't help it. It's a natural instinct for our bears to want to care for our mate. One of the biggest things is to be able to provide a meal for them. It means that we're a good mate because we've taken care of our mate. We honestly don't mean anything else by it." Ryker wrapped his arms around my waist and held me while he looked lovingly into my eyes. "Okay, shall we head to War's? They're expecting us."

I smiled at my One and was still smiling at him when he looked up and realized we were now standing in the same position, only in War and Arik's kitchen.

"Okay, that one was just as good as Edison's. Seriously, I felt just the normal stomach tickle and that's it."

"What can I say? I'm trying. Sometimes I nail it, others, I completely flub it." I shrugged and smiled, resigned to my inabilities at times.

"Sorry, sweetheart. You don't ever flub anything as far as I'm concerned."

"Okay you two lovebirds, since I can hear both of your stomachs growling from over here, why don't you join us for lunch? Since Arik and Elliot were busy showing Aspen around all morning, we're having a late lunch, too," War said while walking into the kitchen. When we looked into the dining room, sure enough, the table was piled with food and my stomach growled, loudly. Ryker looked down at me and glared.

"Yeah, I know. I need to eat. Let go of me and I'll go sit down."

Ryker grabbed my hand and pulled me into the dining room. He went to the opposite end of the table as Aspen and pulled out a chair for me and then took the one right next to me. It made me happy he wanted to sit next to me again.

"I always want to sit next to you, sweetheart. I honestly didn't even notice it last night. And I'm really sorry."

"It's okay. I could have said something, and I didn't, so that's on me."

After piling my plate with food, Ryker sat it in front of me and then gave me a quick kiss before doing the same for himself. We all ate and made small talk over lunch.

"War, shouldn't you be at work?" I asked my brothers mate.

"Gage is covering my lunch shift. He'll go to lunch just as soon as I get back. We're supposed to be getting a new deputy, so that'll be nice. I'll still always be on call no matter what, but it'll be nice to have a third person to rotate shifts with."

After we consumed more food than what one would consider normal for grown men, but not necessarily shifters, we all looked to Papa for his news.

"Aspen, what do you know about the other alpha your parents were talking to?"

"Not much, really. I'd never seen him before. He showed up, had a conversation with my dad one day, then later that night, my parents suggested to me that I needed to leave to find my mate. He showed back up a few days later and got into an argument with my dad. Later that night, my dad told me I had to get out, that it wasn't an option. When I asked him if it was because of the other alpha, he said that Jules had nothing to do with it. That's all I know. Sorry."

"That's okay. So, we went to Alaska this morning to see if we could find out more information for you. When we got to your parent's house, it looked like they'd left in a hurry, and they weren't planning on coming back. When I read the auras in the house, there were those of your parents as well as another alpha. I didn't get a sense of fear but as of right now, I'm not sure where they are or if they're alone or with the other alpha you mentioned," Papa told Aspen. Understandably, Aspen became upset. His parents were missing and Papa hadn't yet been able to locate them.

"We'll keep looking for them, okay? We'd like for you to come back to Alaska with us and let us know if you notice anything."

"Alright," Aspen said as he looked down the table at Ryker. He looked scared, and I didn't blame him. I hoped Aspen got a happy ending and things weren't sounding all that positive at the moment.

Aspen nodded and then the trio were gone again. I immediately looked at Elliot to see if he knew more than what Papa said before leaving with Aspen, and he just subtly shook his head at me.

"Elliot, are you shaking your head no because you're not sure what's going on, or because Aspen's parents didn't make it?"

"It's not good news, Arin. That's why Papa sent you home early. You were already distraught, and he knew he was going to be stepping into a seriously messed up situation."

"What happened?" Ryker asked, the concern apparent in his voice.

"Papa found the bodies of another couple and their son. They weren't Kodiaks so I'm guessing they were traveling through or something. The other aura that surrounded them is one he said he's detected before. At this point, he's not sure what's going on. But given the current circumstances, it's odd they asked Aspen leave to find his mate so suddenly. It's not uncommon to find one's mate away from your birthplace, and it used to be much more common, but in recent times, fated mates have been found closer to home. However, the aura that he detected around the bodies, he believed it's from the group that you detected around your cabin."

Ryker groaned, and I couldn't contain my tears. I'd become incredibly emotional already with pregnancy, but the news Elliot shared was much worse than I ever expected. I looked over at Ryker and he scooted his chair back; I crawled into his lap and silently wept. I'd been pissy with Aspen, and now his parents were missing and not even Papa knew where they were.

"Papa is going to take Aspen home with him for a few days. He's asked that everyone stay as close to home as possible, and if we notice anything odd or concerning, let him know," Elliot told us.

"Are the protection spells still in place?" Ryker asked.

"Yes. You'll be perfectly safe inside your cabin as well as in your immediate back yard. For now though, why don't you take Arin home and cuddle him some more? I can send you two back if you'd like."

"That'd be great. Thanks, Elliot. Troy, could you call Jai and tell him to close up the station and head on home?"

"Already on it. I was calling to tell him to stay put once he got home, anyway," Troy said as he tapped on the screen of his phone and put it up to his ear.

"I'm going to send Gage home, too. I can't exactly close up the sheriff's station, but I'll let dispatch know we've had some sort of sickness come up, or something, and they can reach me on my work cell," War said as he pulled out his own phone.

"That's a good idea. With the station being in town, and the humans there, Papa has to be extra careful around there and can't offer the same level of protection. Ryker, you two ready?" Elliot asked.

I felt Ryker move, but since I was still focused on how upset I was for Aspen, I didn't completely understand that Elliot was transporting us for me. Before I knew it, we were lying down in our bed, back at the cabin.

"Shh. I've got you. Don't worry about Aspen. I know your dads will take care of him."

"I feel so bad for him. His parents are missing and how will we know what happened, really? I don't know if Papa will be able to tell or not."

"Sweetheart, can you honestly say there's something your Papa can't figure out? I don't know Edison very well, but I do know that he's incredibly old and powerful. I'm sure there's a lot that he knows, and can do, that we aren't even aware of."

"You're right. I'm just upset, and I can't seem to stop crying. I'm not supposed to be emotional at this stage, am I?"

"I'm not sure. I know that as a general rule, most things don't follow what's expected when it comes to pregnancies. It's most likely not unusual that you're emotional all of a sudden. You've also had a stressful couple of days. Why don't you try taking a nap and see if that helps?"

"Will you stay here with me?"

"Absolutely. I'll be right here when you wake up. Promise."

"Love you."

"Love you, too."

Ryker gave me a soft, gentle kiss before he pulled away enough to tuck me in his arms. The steady beat of his heart lulled me to sleep like it had so many times in the past couple months. I always felt safe and comfortable in Ryker's arms. It was one of my favorite places to be.

Ryker — 15

Things were touch and go for several days after Edison discovered Aspen's parents missing. Arin was with his brothers at Arik's house, and I was with Troy, War, Edison, and Wallace at the ranger station. Edison had asked to talk to us without our mates.

"Edison, you realize we can't keep anything from our mates, right? They're your sons so why would you not want them here."

"They know a little about what I've discovered; Elliot told you all the other day. If you want them to know everything, that's your choice. But after what happened with Arin a few days ago, I don't want him to become overwhelmed and upset again."

"Are my den members in danger? That's what's most important to me right now. As Alpha, it's my responsibility to ensure everyone in the den is safe."

"Yes, War, everyone is fine. But there will come a time that we will have to defend the den. I'm sorry, but I don't see any other way around that. Troy, son, this will directly affect you in some way. Aspen said the alpha's name is Jules. Does that name ring any bells?"

"I've been thinking about that for the last couple days. The only Jules we had was Sam's younger brother," Troy said.

"Yes. And when I read the auras in the house, Jules was there several times. He was warning Aspen's parents about Alpha Hank's plans to come through Kodiak and kill all of the male omegas."

I looked at Edison with shock. "But that doesn't make sense, we only had the one. Aspen was the only omega in our den, and our den was the only one on the island. All the other children were either females or were alphas, like me."

When Aspen's parents showed up to join our den with a very young Kodiak cub with them, our den welcomed them with open arms. Our Alpha was an asshole, but he wasn't necessarily cruel. And he was more than welcoming to newcomers, no matter what their species was. This issue with same-sex pairings seemed to be a new thing.

Edison continued, speaking directly to me, "From what I could gather about the other family we found, they were from Russia and were passing through. They just happened to be at the wrong place at the wrong time. It was truly a fluke that Alpha Hank happened to see them. But because their son was a male omega, they paid the ultimate price. The readings I was able to get from the house all lead to them wanting to save Aspen. In the end, they saved him by getting him to leave their house. The fact that he ended up at your place and left with you two probably helped. I believe Troy's old Alpha showed up the same night you left with Aspen. He killed the other couple and their son; that could have easily been Aspen and his parents."

My bear and I were both devastated about the lives that were so needlessly taken. At the same time, we were also pissed. Who treated other shifters that way? That wasn't how an Alpha acted.

"I know you're all upset. You three are good alphas and even if your mates weren't male omegas, you'd still have a problem with what's going on. For now, they've moved further away and they're camped in Glacier National Park. Just south of the border. And yes, Alpha Hank is back with them."

"Do you know when they plan on attacking? That is his plan, right?" Troy asked.

"Yes, it is. And yes, I do. You have several months before they'll attack. I'm unsure of why they're waiting, though. They've found what they're looking for," Edison said to us.

"What's that?" War asked.

"Your den is full of male omegas. On top of that, you have a couple that escaped from him once before."

"Sam and Linus?"

"Yes. But he's after Ivan as well. Ivan has a male mate, and he cannot accept that from an alpha."

"So those of us with male mates are all his targets as well? What do we do?" I asked. None of this sounded good. I knew that Hank would be no match for Edison, but I also knew that Edison couldn't just go after him and eliminate the threat without being directly provoked. To do so would conflict with his powers.

"Unfortunately, we wait. The attack won't come until after your baby is born, Ryker. Until then, everything will remain peaceful. But not only are you and your mates to be targeted, your children will be as well."

"There is no way I'm letting that ass-hat near my children. If he thinks...."

"Troy, calm down. I said they are his targets as well. I didn't say he'd ever get near them. And I promise, he won't."

"So it's just business as usual then?" Troy asked. He seemed to calm down considerably, and that was reassuring. I didn't know Edison nearly as well as Troy or War did, but if they weren't overly concerned at the moment, then I wouldn't be either.

"Unfortunately, yes. I know that's not what you three want to hear, but that's the way it has to be. For now, at least."

"And things aren't going to go the way they did with me and Elliot, right?"

"No, Troy. I promise. I'm not using any of you for bait. The attack won't happen until this fall. You have plenty of time to relax and simply love your mates and children," Edison answered.

I'd heard that story, and I would have felt much the same as Troy had in that situation. In the end, it all worked out, but what if it hadn't? I knew Edison would always protect his kids and their mates, but could he always be there? We were interrupted by a knock on the door. When Troy got up to answer, none of us expected to find young Grayson on the other side of the door. He was Ivan and Sam's youngest son who had escaped with his parents and younger sister several months ago.

"Hey, Grayson. Is something wrong?" Troy asked as he stepped back to let the young alpha in.

"It looks like you're in a meeting. I'm sorry, I didn't mean to interrupt. I can come back another time."

"It's okay. We were just finishing up. Is there something I can help you with?" Troy asked.

"Actually, I was hoping to talk to Ryker if I could."

"Sure thing. Why don't we go into my office and we can chat?" I asked while gesturing towards my open office door. Grayson went in, and I looked at the others before I followed him. I remembered Arin mentioning something about dinner so I needed to make sure. "So dinner tonight at War's place, right?"

"Yes. Arik is looking forward to having a dinner with his brothers. Just a head's up, he's going to start bugging you and Arin about having an ultrasound and everything."

"Already done. We scheduled one for Friday. Arin will be just shy of three months so he'll have about two months left to go. Arik said it was the perfect time to do the ultrasound. It's not like we don't already know we're having a warlock. We're getting a little boy and all I care about from here on out is that he's healthy. Arin reassures me each morning that he and the baby are both fine."

"I hope that doesn't upset you, Ryker. He's just trying to keep you up to date on everything happening with him and the baby," Edison told me.

"I know that. I'm not upset. I rather enjoy my morning reports. And I love all of the little kicks and movement."

"Just wait. Although with Arin only having one, I don't think he'll be nearly as miserable as Elliot or Arik were," Troy said.

"True. Arik was ready to cause permanent damage to certain parts of my anatomy when he was two months pregnant," War told us.

"Elliot was just as bad. And he was sick for so long, I felt terrible for him," Troy told me.

"I have to get to the station. I'll see you all later at the house for dinner." War said before he walked out the door.

"We're going to go play with our grandbabies," Edison and Wallace said in unison and then they were gone. I looked at Troy and we both just shrugged our shoulders.

"Let me know if you need anything, but I'm pretty sure I already know what Grayson wants to talk to you about," Troy said before he walked off to his desk without giving me any idea. I got up and went to my office to see what I was wanted for.

"Sorry to keep you waiting. What can I do for you?"

"I'll just come out with it. I want a job. I used to volunteer up at Arctic National Wildlife Refuge until I was old enough to get a paying job there. I've completed my two-year degree, but I'm still working on my bachelor's degree. All I've ever wanted was to be a park ranger. My bear doesn't like to be cooped up, but he's okay as long as I'm outside. I'd prefer to stay in the area, but if I have to, I'll relocate."

"Grayson, how old are you?"

"I just turned twenty-one. I know I'm young, but I know this is what I want to do. Can you help me? I love my parents, but if I don't get out of their house soon, I'll go crazy. But I can't really justify it if I don't even have a job. They want me to finish school first, but Da is driving me crazy. Papa keeps after him, but just like always, he usually doesn't listen."

I opened my desk drawer and pulled out the information sheet he'd need and handed it to him.

"Here's the information. You'll need to go online and fill out all of the paperwork. If you want to stay here, make sure you mark our park as your desired station assignment. Once all of the paperwork is complete, I'll get a message from the regional office, letting me know there's an application for the area. I'm willing to give it a try and see how things work out, but you have to fill out all of the paperwork. You think you can do that?"

"Yes, I can. Thank you, Ryker. I'll go home and get started as soon as I can."

"Also, have you talked to War about one of the cabins out behind his place? I know there's a smaller one that is just a one room cabin. It only has a loft for a bedroom and only one bathroom. It'd be perfect for a single, young, alpha."

"Do you think he'd be willing to let me stay there? I mean, I don't have a job that pays yet and I'm me."

"Grayson, just because you're Ivan and Sam's son, doesn't mean anyone in this den has any issues with you. Or your parents for that matter. What happened fifty years ago couldn't be controlled. Ivan is Sam's fated mate. That's how things work. Nobody holds any ill feelings about what happened."

"I don't know, Ryker. Sometimes I feel like they look at me funny."

"I think that's all in your head. Think about what I said and go talk to War. I'm sure he'd be more than willing to let you stay there. And be sure to fill out that paperwork. The whole process takes a couple weeks, and we could use another ranger around here."

"Thanks, Ryker. I'll swing by the sheriff's station on my way home."

I nodded at the young man and watched as he turned and left my office. I hoped he actually filled everything out. I'd be nice to have another ranger around here. Especially one that was a shifter, and we wouldn't have to be super careful around.

"Hey, what'd Grayson want?"

"Actually, a job."

"No kidding? That'd be nice."

"I was just thinking the same thing. Especially with you having young cubs and me with a pregnant mate."

"Yeah. He did have a funny look on his face when he left though. I just figured you said something to him."

"I don't know about what. I simply handed him the paperwork to apply for a position. Although, I did talk to him about seeing if he could stay at the small cabin at War's. It'd be perfect for a young alpha. Especially one without a mate."

"Oh hey, yeah. It really would. I had hoped that maybe Orin would move into it, but he seems happy and content over with Forrest at the wolf pack. Do you know when Jai is supposed to be back?"

"Well, since we just sent him off yesterday, I would imagine he'll be gone for a week, so probably sometime next week. Why do you ask?"

"No reason in particular. I was just asking."

"With what we learned this morning, and Jai being an omega, I'm actually happier with him not being here. I may not be Alpha here, but I still don't want anything to happen to anyone in the den."

"You and me both," Troy said in agreement. He nodded before getting up and heading back out to his desk to finish his paperwork.

Arin — 16

"Arin, I'm really sorry. I honestly didn't think anything of it. I would never dream of coming between you and Ryker. I realize how it seems, but I was excited to see my old friend and relieved to not have to figure out where to go on my own."

I couldn't help it, I rolled my eyes, again. Aspen had been apologizing to me for a couple days now, and no matter how many times I told him it was okay, he wouldn't listen. He was convinced I was still upset.

"Aspen, listen. This will be the absolute last time I tell you that it's okay. Yes, I was upset that night. I was tired and cranky. It happens. Especially since I'm pregnant and moody. But I felt bad about it the very next day, and I've already apologized to Ryker. Luckily for me, he's a saint and puts up with me."

Aspen smiled at me, and before I could guess his intentions, he was wrapped around me and giving me a tight bear hug. I felt bad for him. He'd left his home without much choice and then found out his parents were probably murdered simply because they had a male omega for a son. The only person he knew was Ryker, who I kept occupied. My papa scared the crap out of him, and yet, he was basically forced to stay with him for the past several days.

"You know, your dads are really cool. And all the neat things Edison can do, it's really amazing."

What was I saying about my parents scaring him? Wow, what a difference a few days can make.

"Okay, the last time I saw you, you were crawling, backwards, away from my papa. What happened?"

"I got to know him? I've honestly never been near a warlock before. We don't exactly have them up in Alaska. But Edison isn't a normal warlock, is he?"

"No, he's not. But he'd never hurt you. I'm sure you're aware of that by now."

"I am. And I'm having so much fun playing with all of the babies. Don't you just want a bunch of babies? I've never seen so many cubs at once before."

"I love my nephews, but I'm super excited about my little guy here."

"I'll bet. Maybe I'll find my mate some day and we can have a cub."

"Maybe. It seems that once War and Arik found each other, everyone else in the den is finding their mates. Before long, the den will be packed full with new mates and cubs. I know War is excited about the prospect."

"Yeah. Arik was saying yesterday that there was another couple from Colorado that were seeking sanctuary."

"It's so sad that they feel they have to. He hasn't said anything to me about it yet. Did they have a male omega child?"

"No, she was a little girl. Cute little thing. But the couple was a male pair. I guess they were starting to feel uncomfortable in their old den."

"That's too bad. It's not like we don't have enough problems with us already being shifters and warlocks. Add in the issues with same-sex mates, and it really shouldn't be an issue. It's not like they had a choice in it. Not really. Fate decided who their mate would be. I remember when I saw Ryker the first time. I'd felt him around before, but never anywhere close by. But he growled and came after me and I was so scared, I teleported away. I felt awful after the fact and I went and found him later that night, but still. The feelings of being near my fated mate are unlike any I can ever come close to describing. And for warlocks, it's different than with shifters. We feel the auras of others, but the aura of our fated One causes intense vibrations in our bodies. With those that aren't our fated One, it's more of a soft hum."

Aspen sighed and I looked over at him and smiled. He was older than me, but not by much.

"Hey, Aspen. Are you ready?" Arik asked as he walked into the room. Since I had no clue as to what they were talking about, I just looked at my twin and raised an eyebrow.

"You didn't know? I was going to show Aspen the little cabin out back. It's super small and is only just one room with a loft, but it's perfect for a single bear."

"Oh hey, that sounds great. Can I come too?"

"Absolutely. Come on. It's just out at the edge of the property. It's really perfect because you can just strip in the cabin, walk out the back door and then you're already at the woods for a run."

"That does sound nice. Your dads' cabin is much the same. Wallace took me out for a run yesterday, and it was nice. I've never seen a tiger before either," Aspen said.

"Well, at least we're expanding your experiences."

When we got to the cabin, we were met by War and Grayson. They were both smiling and walking around the cabin. "Hello, kitten. What are you three doing here? Where are the twins?"

"They're napping and Linus is in the house listening for them for me. I was just going to show Aspen the cabin. I thought it'd be perfect for him."

The look on War's face was almost comical. "Umm, kitten, I just told Grayson he could have the cabin. I'm sorry, Aspen. I didn't realize you wanted your own place. I'm beginning to think we need to build more cabins."

"Don't worry about it, War. Edison and Wallace have made it clear that they are in no hurry for me to leave. And I get to play with all of the boys, too. And with yours and Arik's kids crawling, it's super fun." By the smile on Aspen's face, I knew he meant it.

War and Arik both groaned in unison. I loved my nephews, all five of them, but now that Harrison and Bradley were crawling they were into absolutely everything. I couldn't help but smile at them.

"Just you wait. You'll be in our shoes before you know it," Arik said to me.

"I'm sure I have a while to wait. I'm still pregnant, remember?"

"Oh yeah, that reminds me. Do you think you can talk Ryker into having the ultrasound tonight after dinner?" Arik asked.

"Umm, probably, why?"

"Whatever he's about to tell you, don't listen, Arin. He just wants to see the baby," War said as he smiled down at my twin. War adored my brother, and I was so happy they'd found each other.

"War, are you sure it's okay for me to have the cabin? I mean, I can always stay with my parents. Aspen doesn't have that option."

"Really, it's okay. I don't mind staying with Edison and Wallace. Their cabin is big, and they've made me feel very welcome," Aspen told Grayson while smiling at him.

"You know what it is, right? Arin is mated now and even though he's still learning to master all of his powers, they don't have any kids left at home. We're all mated and starting families of our own. Dad and Papa have empty-nest syndrome." Arik laughed as he said it, but as I thought about it, it was probably true. And right now, Aspen could use the comfort our dads were offering. Up until recently, he still lived with his parents.

"Wow, you're probably right. I never thought about that," I told my twin.

"Hey, if your dads want to adopt me, I'm all for it. Edison is still intimidating, but they're pretty cool." Aspen was trying to be positive, but yet I could tell he was hurting for his parents. It had to be difficult to not know what was going on with them. I got a brief glimpse of the sadness I knew he was feeling about the entire situation, and it made me feel for Aspen.

We all chuckled at Aspen and turned to walk back to the main house. But I knew he was hurting more than he let on.

"Grayson, if you want the cabin, it's yours. If you need me to talk to your dads, I can do that."

"As much as I appreciate the offer, I should be the one to tell them I'm moving out. But thanks, Alpha. I really appreciate it. Now all I have to do is get the job with Ryker."

"Oh? Do you need help with that?" I asked. Ryker had mentioned it briefly through our bond earlier, but I didn't have all of the details."

"Thanks, Arin, but that's not necessary. Ryker said I had to fill out all of the paperwork. I just have to get to it and get it finished. That's all."

"So you don't need Arin to distract him while he's approving your application?" Arik asked, teasingly.

"No," Grayson replied but looked down at the ground. The fact that he blushed reminded me that he was super young, and just a few months ago, I was just as innocent as he was. Hopefully, he found a mate to have cubs with. I was mated and pregnant and still I blushed at most things. Even the thought of what Arik suggested had me shooting daggers my twin's way.

"War, you've corrupted my brother," I said as I turned the daggers towards my brother-in-law.

"Arin, I have no problems with that," War said as he scooped Arik up, and threw him over his shoulder, before he took off running towards the house.

"Well, I guess that means supper is going to be on us, Aspen. Grayson, would you like to stay for dinner?"

"Thanks, but no. I want to get home and fill out the paperwork. Hopefully, I can get it all completed tonight and your mate will have it soon. My bear has started getting antsy, and I just want to be able to be out in the woods. It helps keep him calm and mellow."

"Maybe you could talk to Troy about that. I know he has a couple places that he goes where he can shift. He knows where's safe and where isn't. And if you ever need to, one of us could take you back to Alaska so you can shift and swim in the sea. Elliot and Troy go up to their cabin there a lot. It's not too far from the water, and Troy always seems more mellow after he's spent a day or two up there and has been able to shift."

"Thanks, Arin. I appreciate it. I'll talk to him for sure. For now, I just want to see if maybe getting out of the house and away from my Da will help. I love him, but at times, he just doesn't seem to get it."

"We're here for you if you ever need us. And I mean that. We're not alphas like the others, but if you need anything, just let us know. And if I can't help you, I'll get Ryker or Troy, or even Dad. And we can always talk to Papa, he could have you dropped in the Bering Sea in about two seconds if you wanted."

"Thanks, Arin. I really appreciate that. I have to get home. I have Papa's car, and I've already been gone a little longer than I said I'd be."

"Okay. Just remember what I said, Grayson."

"I will."

Grayson turned and walked around the side of the house. I watched him go and once he was out of sight, I turned to Aspen who was also watching Grayson's retreating form."

"Not your mate, huh?"

"I wish. He's a lot younger than me, but he's cute."

I chuckled at that but had to agree. Grayson was cute. But he was nothing like Ryker. He was it for me. Period.

"Okay, shall we go figure out supper? War will have Arik stuck on his knot for the next hour, at least. I don't know about you, but I'm hungry. And when I get hungry, Ryker always seem to know and suddenly appears and starts shoving food at me."

Aspen started laughing, and when I looked up, I realized why. There was Ryker and I knew he'd heard me. When he motioned for me to come to him, I rolled my eyes and let go of Aspen's arm and walked to my mate. I knew I was about to spend the next few minutes being fussed over. Not that I really minded. Because I didn't. I loved that Ryker was always fussing over me. What can I say, my One was the most important person to me, and the fact that he doted on me wasn't a hardship.

"What's this I hear about you being hungry? Why didn't you eat?"

"I ate lunch. I just skipped my snack."

Ryker did his best to look stern, but it didn't work. I could tell he wasn't upset, but I also knew he only wanted what was best for me.

"Hi there. Don't I even get a kiss?" I asked. Ryker immediately melted and wrapped me up in his arms, my absolute favorite place to be. When he gave me a sweet kiss, I remembered that we weren't alone and there would be time for other kisses later.

"Mmm, I like how you think, sweetheart. But right now, you know my bear wants you fed. At least a small snack."

"I know. I have no problems with that."

I smiled at my One, and he wrapped his arm around my shoulders before he turned us to head inside.

"Come on, Aspen. You can keep us company while I figure out what my mate wants to eat. It seems to change on a daily basis," Ryker said over his shoulder. He was right though. It did seem to continually change. Arik said the only thing he ever craved was hoagie sandwiches. And not small ones. Elliot couldn't eat much of anything simply because he didn't have room. Luckily for me, I was only having one baby and my bump was still what my brothers called disgustingly cute and adorable. I laughed at them but knew I probably shouldn't. Knowing my luck, I'd end up with multiples next time if the fates blessed us with more children. We all went into War and Arik's kitchen to raid the pantry and catch up on the day's events.

Ryker — 17

Dinner with Arin's brothers and their mates was always a wonderful time. It was loud, funny, and just made me feel good. I didn't have siblings so dinnertime in my house was always a quiet affair, but not here, not when you had Elliot, Arik, and Arin together. We laughed and talked about the trouble the twins got into growing up, and Wallace and Edison were right there to add to the stories. It was good to see Aspen having fun and feeling so at home with our little group.

Harrison was determined he was going to be the center of attention and kept shouting from his high chair. I had to chuckle at that. He was going to be a handful in about fifteen years.

"I know what you're thinking over there, and you're absolutely right. But just you wait, you're having a little warlock. Just imagine a much younger version of your mate," War told me. I knew he didn't mean anything by it, but I still wanted to defend my mate.

"I love the idea of a little version of Arin running around. And if the fates are kind enough, several more," I said as I looked over at my little warlock. I couldn't wait to hopefully have a house full of children with him. As many as he and the fates were willing to give us, I was all for it.

My thoughts were interrupted by Harrison screaming from his highchair. Arik wasn't feeding him fast enough, and he glared at War who seemed to be the only person that their older twin responded to. Well, War and Wallace; that boy was one hundred percent alpha and he knew it. After handing War the jar of baby food and wiping his hands, Arik turned to us and asked the question I'd been waiting for.

"Okay, so what do you say to doing the ultrasound now?"

"What happened to Friday?"

"Yeah, well, about that..." Arik trailed off, looking embarrassed.

I laughed at my mate's twin and his mate, who was doing his best to try to look busy. Unfortunately for him, the jar of baby food was now empty and Harrison was content to just sit in his highchair and look at the adults at the table.

"Don't let them try and fool you. They've somehow managed to convince Edison and I to watch the twins for them this weekend. They're wanting to go away without the twins and were hoping to leave Friday morning."

"Well, why didn't you just say so?" Arin asked.

"Because I'd already made plans to do your ultrasound before War came and asked me to go away for the weekend. I really want to go, Arin. Harrison and Bradly are nine months old now, and we haven't had a weekend away without them."

"You don't have to convince me. I'm all for it. Whereas Arin can sense and hear our little guy, I can't. Not really. I can hear his heartbeat, but not the same way Arin can. If you're willing to do the ultrasound now, my only question is why are we still sitting here in the dining room?" What can I say? I was anxious to see my little guy.

"Alright, Arin. Your One is anxious to see the little one. What do you say?" Arik asked.

"I'm all for it so let's go. War, since you had my brother otherwise occupied while he was supposed to be helping me and Aspen with dinner, you're on cleanup duty," Arin said as he walked away from the table. When I glanced at War, he was trying his best to not laugh out loud, he was about to fail, miserably though.

"Okay, Arin. It's super simple. You just need to climb up on the table and then get comfortable. In hopes that you'd say yes, I turned on the warmer earlier so hopefully the gel isn't too cold."

Arin climbed up on the table and laid down. I sat beside him and grabbed his hand that he offered me. I was both nervous, as well as excited.

"Ryker, it's okay. He's just fine," my mate told me. I looked into his blue eyes and fell in love all over again.

"I know. I'm just excited."

"If I'd thought about it, I would have had you come in last month, and you could've seen him. I'm sorry, Ryker."

"Why? You're busy. And there's been a lot going on the last couple months."

"True. But still. I know what it's like to be anxious about seeing your baby. When I was pregnant with the twins, I couldn't wait to see them. Neither could War."

Arik raised Arin's shirt and then squirted some blue gel all over his stomach. He still had the cutest little bump, and I just couldn't get over it. To anyone in the shifter world, they would be able to tell he was pregnant. If a human happened to see him, he'd look like a tall, skinny guy with an odd beer belly.

When Arik moved a gray thing that looked like a computer mouse all over Arin's stomach, I watched in fascination as the blank screen on the monitor suddenly came to life with images of our baby. But when he reached over and hit a button on the keyboard, the room was suddenly filled with the swish-swish sounds of the baby's heartbeat. My eyes left the screen and flew to meet my mate's.

"That's our baby. That's our little guy's heartbeat. It sounds so different. Oh wow," I said. I couldn't help it, I became incredibly emotional and started to cry. Out of nowhere, Arin handed me a box of tissues. "Thanks, sweetheart."

"I'd do anything for you, Ryker. You should know that by now."

"And I would do the same for you, sweetheart." I gave Arin a quick kiss and then looked back at the monitor. Arik was drawing circles and lines on the screen and pushing a bunch of buttons on the keyboard. He was in his zone and completely focused on what he was doing. After several minutes, he looked up at us and smiled.

"He looks great you two. He's very healthy and is quite large for his age. You have a very solid baby there, and he's doing great. His growth is good. You two have nothing to worry about as of now. I know you worry, Ryker, but really, this little guy looks amazing." Arik grabbed a towel and wiped off Arin's stomach and then pulled down his shirt. I helped him sit up, and when Arik handed us a sheet of little black and white pictures, I couldn't keep from crying again.

"Thank you, Arik. These are wonderful."

"Awe, it's okay, Ryker. War loves the ultrasound pictures we have of the twins. And Troy's the same way."

"I know. He has one in a frame on his desk at work. He also has pics of the five of them that were taken right after they were born. I'm sure that'll be me as well."

"There is nothing wrong with that. War's the same way. Have you seen his desk at work? I often wonder how he gets anything done with all of the pictures he has of me and the twins on it."

I smiled at Arik and then looked at my mate who was looking at the pictures and silently crying. My mate mark had started to throb, and I knew I needed to get him home and give him the attention he needed. After the evening we'd brought Aspen home with us, he hadn't denied himself his needs. I made sure he knew I was always willing to give him anything I could. Especially if it was something as simple as being knotted to him for an hour or two.

"You ready to head home?"

Arin looked up at me and blushed. I was only as experienced as he was, but for whatever reason, he was still quite shy about everything. Edison said it was because he was a warlock and had only ever been around Wallace and Arik, as far as shifters go, while growing up. Give it time, and he'd be just as uninhibited as Arik.

"Yeah. Is that okay? It's been a long, busy day."

"Of course, it is. Why don't we go show everyone the pictures of our little guy, and we can go home and discuss names or something?"

"Oh, we're going to have to name him, aren't we?"

I chuckled at that because that was just about all I'd thought about for the past several days. I had several suggestions, but I wanted Arin to have an equal say in naming our son.

"Okay, you two. I'm sure Dad and Papa are ready to see the pictures. If you two don't get out there, they'll probably barge in here soon. Ryker, here is a second set of pictures for you. Now you can be just like War and Troy and have tons of pictures on your desk at work."

"Thanks so much, Arik. I'll have to go shopping for some frames, but these are perfect."

After helping Arin off of the table—because that's just what I did even if he didn't need help—we walked out of the room while Arik stayed behind and cleaned up the equipment. Sure enough, we were descended upon just as soon as we entered the kitchen.

After several minutes of oohing over the pictures, I was almost ready to cry. All I wanted to do was get my mate home and take care of him.

"Sweetheart, is there any way we can get out of here without embarrassing you?"

"Hmm, well, I guess I could start yawning, but since I'm only in my second trimester, they're not going to buy that."

"Then that won't work. Any other suggestions?"

"Yeah, how about this one?"

Arin looked up at me, smiled, looked at our family and simply said "Bye everyone." And then we were home in our own cabin. Not only were we finally home, we were in our bedroom, naked, and Arin had a look on his face that I hadn't seen before. I had a feeling I was going to enjoy tonight.

The vibrations in my mate mark were almost painful for me so I knew that Arin had to be in pain.

"Are you okay, sweetheart?"

"Yes. Just very horny. You might want to send Troy a message and let him know that you're probably not going to be in to work on time tomorrow morning."

My shock must have shown on my face because Arin chuckled and then crawled onto our bed and started slowly stroking his hard cock. I growled and quickly climbed on top of him and gently batted his hands away.

"Mine," I said before I pushed Arin's legs up so I could get at his leaking hole. I licked up from his hole to the tip of his leaking cock and then after swirling my tongue around the crown, I sucked it down, all the way to the root.

"Ryker. Yes! More. I need more."

"What do you need, sweetheart?" I asked when I pulled off long enough to talk but went right back to sucking my mate's cock. I was rewarded with a burst of salty liquid, and it caused me to moan at the same time Arin did.

Arin panted above me, and when I thrust two fingers into him, he shouted and filled my mouth with his release. That was the 'more' he needed, but I wasn't finished with him yet. I continued to thrust my fingers in and out of him while his cock released more of the salty liquid I couldn't get enough of.

"Ryker, please," Arin begged. I pulled my fingers from his hole and after licking them clean, I flipped him over and filled him in one thrust. "Yes! More. I need more," Arin pleaded with me. I didn't want to hurt him so I made long, steady strokes in and out of his slick hole. "No, harder. I need it harder. Please." Arin thrashed and withered on the bed but I just couldn't do what he asked.

"Sweetheart, I don't want to hurt you or the baby."

"You won't. But I need it harder. Please."

I gave Arin one forceful thrust and he groaned, and his hole clamped down on me causing my knot to start to swell. "Sweetheart, I'm not going to be able to move much longer if you keep squeezing me like that."

"Don't care. More. Give me more just like that. Almost there," Arin begged in front of me. When he sent me images of the days after we'd first claimed each other, and he was in his very first fertile cycle, I lost it and gave in. I grabbed his hips and started pounding into him as hard and fast as I could.

"Yes! Ryker!" Arin shouted as his channel clamped down on my cock, and my knot completely filled and I couldn't move any more. It started pulsing inside him, filling him with my seed once again. I pulled his shoulders up, and instead of kissing him like I intended, I bit down on his claiming mark once again. He screamed and just as he started painting the blanket in front of us with another orgasm, I felt a searing burn on my chest where my mate mark was. When I collapsed, turning us both on our sides, I expected to land on the soft bed in front of us, but instead, we landed on the hard floor. The floor of my childhood home in Alaska.

Arin — 18

"Arin, sweetheart. We're in Alaska. Why are we in Alaska?"

"Mmm, more, Ryker. Please," I begged. There was something going on with my body that I didn't quite understand. I'd been horny before, and I was warned about the second trimester rivaling my fertile periods, but I didn't fully understand the way my body was feeling.

"Sweetheart, can you get us back to Montana?"

"Huh?" I asked as I looked around. "Where are we? This place looks familiar."

"It's my house in Alaska. Can you teleport us back to the cabin in Montana, or should I carry you upstairs?"

"So sleepy, Ry. Please." I drifted off to gentle kisses to the back of my neck and Ryker's deep chuckle in my ear. I remember feeling like I was floating and then a deep, warm sleep.

When I woke up the next morning, the sun was shining bright in the room, but it was a room I'd never been in before. I would have been concerned if not for the fact that Ryker's arms were tightly wrapped around me from behind, and I could feel his breath on my neck.

I shrieked at the sight of a strange couple standing on the other side of the room staring at us. That immediately woke Ryker up, and he woke up with a roar, fangs and claws out and covering my body.

After looking at the couple, he calmed down and asked, "Mom? Dad? What are you doing here?"

"Ryker? Who? What? Where?" Ryker's father asked. If we hung around a little longer, maybe he'd get around to asking why and how as well. Ryker's parents kept looking up at Ryker and then down at me, then back to their son. I pulled the blanket further up my body and did my best to hide under it. Ryker looked around the room and then down at me and then back at his parents.

"Would you two kindly leave? We'd like to get dressed if you don't mind."

"If you'd picked a shifter for a bed partner instead of—"

"Do *not* finish that sentence father. You two don't live here anymore, and you will *not* speak to my mate like that. Out. Now."

At Ryker's growl, his mother squeaked and both of his parents ran for the bedroom door. Once it was closed, Ryker laid back down behind me and wrapped me back up in his arms.

"Good morning, sweetheart. How are you this morning? I don't suppose you could lock that door, could you?"

I glanced at the door and then with a thought, the lock clicked into place. Ryker sighed behind me, and I couldn't wait to ask him the questions I had.

"Good morning. Is it morning? It doesn't feel like it. And why are we in Alaska? What happened?"

"Sweetheart, I think we need to talk to your Papa. Especially if you don't remember last night. Is it possible that you can get us some clothes? And maybe my phone?"

"Yeah, sure," I said as I sat up and then Ryker's phone and a set of clean clothes for each of us appeared at the end of the bed.

"Okay, so it's almost lunchtime in Montana. So yeah, not noon here in Alaska. Would you like to take a shower with me, or do you want to do your thing and take care of that for us?"

Deciding that we could always soak in a tub, or take a long, hot shower later, I had us both clean and dressed in a blink. Ryker looked down at himself and then back up at me and smiled.

"I don't know about you, but your son is pushing on my bladder right at the moment, and I really need the bathroom. Where is it?"

"Oh, yeah. It's that door right behind you. You go ahead and take care of business, and I'll call Troy and let him know I'm going to be late."

"Aren't you a little late in doing that?"

"Yeah, which is why I need to call him. Go ahead and take care of whatever you need to, and I'll be in to do the same in just a few."

"Alright. I love you," I said as I got up off of the large bed.

"Love you, too, sweetheart," Ryker said as I walked to the bathroom. I closed the door and could hear him mumbling as I relieved my full bladder. When the door opened behind me, Ryker walked over to me and when I was finished up, he did the same. We both washed our hands and then when we left the bathroom, there was Papa sitting on the bed we'd just been in. He was the last person I expected to see. I looked up at Ryker who just smiled and shrugged his shoulders.

"Papa? What are you doing here?"

"Shouldn't I be asking you that question? Troy said you two were here and that you needed me," Papa said as he looked at Ryker.

"I thought it might be best. We were...umm, last night when..."

Papa laughed before shaking his head at my One. Yeah, telling someone like Edison Whitmore that you were getting busy with his son the night before could be a little uncomfortable.

"You two. Okay, so since I know what you're talking about let's just skip the part where you were busy and get to the part where you two ended up here in Alaska."

"Yeah, so, umm...Arin was really into it last night, and when I gave in and everything, I sort of bit him on his claiming bite again and when I did, I felt a searing burn on my mating mark again. When I laid us both down, we were on the floor downstairs and not on our bed at home in Montana. I asked Arin to take us back home, but he fell asleep. We were knotted together so I carried him upstairs and then we woke up just a little while ago. He doesn't seem to remember brining us here, and I'm a little worried. That's why I wanted Troy to call you."

Papa looked at us and smiled. "It's really nothing to worry about. I think you're probably going to need a lot of time off for the next month or so though. For whatever reason, the normal benefits of Arin's second trimester seem to have hit him a little later than expected and are a whole lot more intense. Tell me, Ryker, why did you bite him again?"

"Honestly, I don't know. I've never bitten him before, except to claim him. I promise, I won't do it again."

"Why would you promise that? Neither of you probably want to hear it, but Wallace and I thoroughly enjoy it when he bites me during orgasm. As for the pain you felt in your mate mark, it was just the direct response to the pain that Arin felt in his mark. It didn't hurt anything and it won't hurt you. You two will get used to what you want to do and don't want to do. But remember this, whatever you two do in the bedroom, or wherever else, there's nothing wrong with it. Each couple is different and each couple enjoys different things. But as long as you are both in agreement, there's nothing wrong with what goes on between you. Understand?"

"Yes, Papa," I said and I felt Ryker nod behind me.

"Great. Now, do you need me to stay with you while you talk to your parents? I think that in some subconscious way, Arin knew your parents were back here and either wanted to meet them or thought you would want to see them. That's why he brought you here. I can't know for sure unless Arin lets me read his aura."

"It's okay. I don't mind being here. It's not the first time that Arin's teleported us while we were…busy."

Papa chuckled and I turned red. I knew there was nothing to be embarrassed about, but it was uncomfortable talking to him about this.

"You know, Elliot got the nickname firecracker because he kept conjuring his light during sex. Ryker calls you sweetheart, but maybe he should call you *poof*." Papa laughed as he stood up and walked towards us. He gave us both hugs before he smiled and took a step back. "Everything will be just fine. I'll see you two in just a little while. As you know, Troy said to remind you that you don't need to come in today. It's Thursday and slow. He said nothing is going on."

"I know, but with Jai off visiting his parents in California for a week, that only leaves the two of us."

"Yes, but he was planning on putting a note on the door with his phone number and heading home. It's really not tourist season yet, and you three aren't doing a whole lot. Although, young Grayson is going to be a good addition to your team. Especially with everything that's about to happen. Just remember, everything happens for a reason."

With that, Papa was gone and I was left with my One in his bedroom in Alaska.

"Hmm, maybe you should call me poof instead of sweetheart. I'm really sorry about this, Ryker."

"Why? I'm not. And just think, you get to meet my parents. Not that that was something I was pushing for. After all, they are my parents and haven't ever really shown any interest in me so far."

"Yeah, I thought you said they were traveling."

"They were, as far as I knew. They signed the house over to me almost a century ago and just took off. I haven't seen them in close to twenty-five years."

"Wow, I can't imagine not seeing my parents for that long."

"Like I said, they weren't interested in having a family. It's almost unheard of and I can't understand it. They just seemed to want more from life. They raised me, but that's it. They didn't really mistreat me, but they weren't overly affectionate. Once I was old enough to take care of myself, they took off and started traveling. I used to hear from them every so often, but then their calls started getting further apart, and they visited less and less frequently."

"Okay, they're your parents, and for that, I'll love them simply because they gave me you. Without them, I wouldn't have my One. But they sound like really terrible parents."

"True. They are. What do you say we go say hi and I can introduce you to them?"

"Sounds good. Then we can go home and you can feed me."

Ryker growled, which caused me to laugh. I turned around and walked towards the door he had me lock earlier. I guess it was time to meet my in-laws. We hurried down the stairs and when we made it to the kitchen, I got another look at his parents. Ryker was a younger, somewhat leaner version of his father, only he had his mother's sandy-blond hair.

"Hello mother, father. What are you two doing here? And how did you get in?"

"Really, Ryker? That's how you want to greet us after all this time?" Ryker's mother asked, looking exasperated.

"I haven't heard from either of you in over twenty-five years. You haven't returned any of my calls, and I changed the locks a decade ago. This might have been your house at one time, but you signed it over to me. Now tell me how you got in. You're lucky I realized it was you two before I jumped out of bed or before I fully shifted."

"You're not going to introduce us?"

"No, I'm not. You haven't wanted to have much of anything to do with me for almost a century, and you completely cut me off all those years ago. Why should I introduce you to my mate?"

"Mate? Really? You found your mate?" Ryker's mom asked. At the word mate, she seemed hopeful, and when she looked down at my stomach, she smiled and then looked back up at her son. Ryker, on the other hand, pushed me behind him and held me there.

"Sweetheart, can you do that thing that your Papa does where others can't get into the house?"

"Yeah. But we're still in it. Did you want me to wait until after we left?"

"Yes, please. I'm about to send them packing, and I'm through with this. There's just too much going on right now to have to add inattentive parents all of a sudden reemerging into my life. I don't know what's suddenly changed, but I don't like nor trust it."

"Whatever you want, Ryker. I love you and will support any decision you make."

"Love you, too."

Ryker looked at his parents and then growled. "Nope, you don't get to all of a sudden show back up and expect a warm welcome. Go home. Wherever that is, go. You're not welcome here, and you're not welcome anywhere else that we happen to be."

"Ryker. Please. We just want—"

"I said no. Now get out."

I could feel the anger vibrating off of my One, and when I placed my hands on his shoulders, he almost immediately relaxed. I watched realization hit Ryker's parents before they turned and left the house through the open back door. They walked to a truck parked in the driveway, climbed in, and left. I didn't know exactly how to comfort my One so I did the only thing I could think of. I walked around to his front, wrapped my arms around him, and buried my face in his neck.

"Love you so much, Arin. So much," Ryker said as he rocked us back and forth in the kitchen.

Ryker — 19

Seeing my parents a couple months ago brought up both good and bad memories. My parents were never going to win any awards for best parents, but they were still my parents, and I was torn. Especially since I was about to become one myself.

Arin was due any day now, and he was absolutely adorable if you asked me. I couldn't get enough of my mate, and the fact that he had what his brothers both now called an unfair pregnant belly made me laugh. He was pregnant, and it was visible if you looked at him from the side. When you were behind him, you couldn't tell at all. And from the front, it was really hard to tell because he looked as if he was just wearing a baggy shirt. Both Arik and Elliot said it was unfair that Arin wasn't a whale at this point. He laughed at his brothers, and I kept quiet about it.

"Ryker?"

"In the office, sweetheart," I called as my pregnant mate yelled to get my whereabouts.

"There you are. Whatcha doing?"

"Finishing up paperwork. My leave has been approved, and I wanted to make sure everything was finished before I handed the station over to Troy for the next several weeks."

"It's September and the park is full of tourists. Are you sure that's okay? I mean, I understand if you need to go to work."

"I know you do, and that's amazing of you. But I've already discussed everything with Troy and Jai. Besides, Grayson is scheduled to finish up his training next week, and he'll be here in just a couple weeks as a full ranger. I don't know who's more excited about that, him or the rest of us. The park doesn't get a whole lot of tourists, and the numbers have steadily declined over the past decade or so, which is why they cut this station from five to three."

"So how did you get them to agree to a fourth?"

"I told them the truth. Troy has triplets, and I had a baby on the way. We needed another ranger to help with rotations. They agreed."

"Well, that's good. Subject change, sorry. Papa called. He said he and Dad would be here for dinner in a few minutes."

"That's good. Is there a reason why Edison is hanging around more lately?"

"Probably. My biggest question is what do you want for dinner? I haven't even started it but wanted to know what you were in the mood for. I'm not really hungry, but I know you and your bear are going to push me to eat, like always."

"I can't help it. You know this. As for what to make, I really don't have a preference. Why don't we go to the kitchen and see what we can find?"

"Sounds good," Arin said as he turned and walked out the door. When he was no longer in my sight, I realized I was supposed to be following him and quickly got up to do just that. I met him, as well as his dads, in the kitchen. Edison and Wallace smiled at me knowingly. They definitely knew something I didn't know.

"Everything okay?" My first and only concern right now was Arin. I couldn't handle anything happening to my mate. My bear would lose his mind.

"Everything's just fine. It's exactly how it's supposed to be," Edison said just as I felt a sharp pain in my stomach. When I looked at Arin, he was doubled over and holding his stomach. The floor beneath him was completely soaked where his water had broken.

"Papa?" Arin asked as I rushed to my mate and picked him up.

"Ryker, if you could take him up to the bedroom. I've prepared the bed for the birth. This won't take but a few minutes and then you two will be meeting your little one."

I nodded and turned and rushed to the bedroom that we'd shared for the past five months. There was a thick, absorbent-looking blanket on the bed, and I gently laid Arin down on it. The pain I was feeling through our bond was only getting stronger, and I knew it had to be so much more intense for him. I looked at him, and he smiled at me, of all things.

"I love you, Ryker. We're about to be dads. I can't believe that."

"I love you, too, sweetheart. Are you okay? I can feel your pain through our bond."

"I'm fine. But I'm really excited, too."

I smiled down at my mate, my life, and ran my fingers through his hair as Edison and Wallace walked into the room. Arin was naked in a blink and covered by a sheet from the waist down. "Ryker, once I have him cleaned and wrapped up, I'll hand him to you and then you and Arin can gush over him, alright?"

"Sounds good. He's already in a lot of pain, is this going to hurt him even more?"

"Don't worry, I'm about to take care of that," Edison said moments before the pain I was feeling in my stomach eased and Arin sighed in relief. I looked to Edison, worried.

"There's nothing to be concerned about. I've numbed him from the waist down is all. Now, would you like to meet your son?"

I looked at Arin's dads and then back to my mate and ran my hand down the side of his face before answering. "Yes. I think we'd very much like to meet him." My precious mate nodded enthusiastically, and Wallace and I both chucked.

"Alright. Let's begin, shall we?"

I nodded but never took my eyes off of Arin's. Even when our son took his first breath moments later, I never broke eye contact with my mate.

"I love you so much, Arin. Thank you."

"Love you more."

I smiled at my mate that had just made us fathers. Life was so good right now.

"Ryker, would you like to meet your son?" Wallace asked as he walked over to us with a little blue bundle. I gasped when he handed me our son, but I was more than eager to meet the little warlock I'd created with my love.

"He's absolutely beautiful, Arin. Look at how perfect he is." I showed him to my crying mate, and I couldn't help it, I joined him. We'd done that. We'd created the beautiful little baby in my arms.

"Have you two decided on a name?" Wallace asked as he smiled at us. Arin couldn't stop touching his tiny little face.

"We have. We decided on Edwin Charles," Arin told his dads. They both gasped and I smiled. I was in complete agreement with him about naming our son after his dads' fathers. When I looked at my fathers-in-law, Edison was closing up Arin's incision and Wallace was staring at the baby, crying.

"Thank you. That's a beautiful thing for you two to do," Wallace said as he placed his hands on his mate's shoulders. Edison was finishing up his task, but when he looked up at me and smiled, he too had tears in his eyes and running down his cheeks.

"You're welcome, but really, it's all on Arin. I was pretty much clueless when it came to names and was happy with whatever Arin wanted."

"Only because you wanted to call him Cortez!" Arin said while rolling his eyes. I just winked at Edison and Wallace before returning my attention back to my mate.

"What can I say? You're so much better at naming our children. I'll try to come up with a better name next time."

Arin narrowed his eyes at me before he looked back at our son in my arms.

"You ready to hold him?" I asked. I already knew the answer, but I was unsure if he'd be able to sit up just yet.

"Yes, but can you just lay him on my chest. And maybe put a pillow behind me?"

"We're going to go let everyone else know that Edwin has arrived. We'll be downstairs if you need us. You two get to know your son."

"You sure you don't want to hold him first, Papa?"

"I'll have plenty of time to hold him later. Right now, you two meet and bond with your son. Just shout if you need us."

"Thanks, Papa."

"Yes. Thank you for everything, Edison. You too, Wallace. I really appreciate all that you two have done for us."

"Son, that's what family does. Now enjoy your new bundle of joy," Edison said as he and Wallace got up and walked out of the bedroom. I gently placed our son on Arin's chest and then rearranged the pillows behind him. He cooed and smiled at our little one. Once I had Arin situated, I kicked off my shoes and gently crawled into bed beside my mate and son.

"He's absolutely beautiful, Arin. Thank you for such a precious treasure," I said as I kissed first Arin's temple and then the top of the blue hat that Edison had placed on Edwin's head. Our son was fast asleep, all warm and cozy on his Papa's chest.

"I wouldn't have him without you, so thank you. He's perfect, Ryker. I can't get over how tiny he seems. I swear, with the way he's been pushing on my bladder for the past month, I figured he'd be so much bigger."

"He's exactly the size he's supposed to be, sweetheart."

Arin couldn't contain the yawn that escaped him, and I quickly wrapped him up in my arms and snuggled my little family. I laid there and listened to the soft snores of my mate and just watched our son sleep. Our peace would soon end once the rest of our family arrived to meet the newest member of our den.

"Ryker, I promise it's okay. You're only going to be gone for a little while. But you should really be there for Grayson's first day on the job."

"Sweetheart, you only had Edwin two weeks ago. Maybe you're ready to get rid of me, but I'm not ready to go back to work yet."

"I didn't say anything about you spending the entire day at work. But really, if you're gone for an hour, it's okay. Besides, you just fed Edwin. He's going to sleep for the next couple hours. You know this."

"I know. How did we get such a calm child?"

"Don't question it, just be happy."

"I'm more than happy. Alright, would you mind poofing me to the station? It's so much quicker, and I'll let you know when I'm ready to come home."

"You know I don't mind. Tell everyone hello for me, will you?"

"I will. I love you and I'll see you soon. If you need me, just bring me back home, okay?"

"Absolutely."

I gave our son one last kiss and handed him off to my mate. I loved seeing him with our son in his arms. It made my bear both proud and happy. He was preening with glee at our son's arrival, and when we introduced Edwin to him for the first-time last week, my bear was beside himself with joy.

Before I could argue further, Arin had me at the ranger station and Troy shook his head at me.

"I can't believe you actually left that little gem of yours."

"I know. It's already tearing me apart, but Arin insisted that I be here to welcome Grayson for his first day."

"It makes sense, but I don't think I could have left Elliot and the triplets this soon."

"I'm not staying long. Where's Jai?"

"I'm right here," he said as he walked up behind me with a fresh cup of coffee in his hand.

"Oh, coffee. That sounds good," I said as I heard a car door close. When it was almost immediately followed by a loud growl, then a coffee mug shattering as it hit the hardwood floor, Troy and I immediately locked eyes and smiled. We both slowly turned and looked at the door that had been thrown open with a loud bang before we lost it and started laughing. There stood Grayson, our newest ranger, but he wasn't even looking at us. Nope, he was staring down Jai.

The End

Connect with Taylor!

Thank you so much for reading Ryker's Enchantment. I hope you enjoyed it! Up next in the Honey Creek Den series will be Grayson and Jai's story.

Want to know when my next book is being released? How about giveaways and sales?

You can find me on Facebook here:
https://www.facebook.com/profile.php?id=100016810573958

My reader group is here:
https://www.facebook.com/groups/729846413870305

You can find me on Instagram here:
https://www.instagram.com/author_taylor_rylan/

You can find me on Twitter here:
https://twitter.com/TaylorRylan1

You can visit my web page here:
www.taylorrylan.com

All signed paperbacks can be found there in the store.

Join my newsletter here:

http://eepurl.com/dtBOKz

I promise not to spam you or ever sell your email address to anyone. My newsletter will be used solely for marketing and announcements about upcoming releases and sales.

Feel free to contact me! I would love to hear from you.

If you enjoyed this book, please consider leaving a review on Amazon. It doesn't have to be long; any review helps indie authors like me. The more reviews we get, the better chance we have of Amazon promoting our books for us! Thank you!

Current List of Books

Shifters/MPREG

Honey Creek Den Series

War's Mate

https://mybook.to/WarsMate

Troy's Warlock

https://mybook.to/TroysWarlock

Ryker's Enchantment

https://mybook.to/RykersEnchantment

Contemporary Series

Men of Crooked Bend Series

My Forever, My Always: Men of Crooked Bend Book 1

https://mybook.to/MFMAebook

My Choice, My Chance: Men of Crooked Bend Book 2

https://mybook.to/MCMCebook

My Survivor, My Savior: Men of Crooked Bend Book 3

https://mybook.to/MSMSebook

My Truth, My Future: Men of Crooked Bend Book 4

https://mybook.to/MTMFebook

My Heat, My Home: Men of Crooked Bend Book 5

https://mybook.to/MHMHebook

My Love, My Valentine: A Men of Crooked Bend Companion Novel (4.5)

https://mybook.to/MLMVebook

Made in the USA
Middletown, DE
23 September 2018